THE RIVALS
OF ACADIA

MORE WILDSIDE CLASSICS

Please see www.wildsidepress.com for a complete list!

THE RIVALS OF ACADIA

AN OLD STORY OF THE NEW WORLD

HARRIET
VAUGHAN CHENEY

WILDSIDE PRESS

THE RIVALS OF ACADIA

This edition published 2005 by Wildside Press, LLC.
www.wildsidepress.com

When two authorities are up,
Neither supreme, how soon confusion
May enter 'twixt the gap of both, and take
The *one by the other*.
SHAKSPEARE.

CHAPTER I.

Far on th' horizon's verge appears a speck —
A spot — a mast — a sail — an armed deck!
Their little bark her men of watch descry,
And ampler canvas woos the wind from high.

LORD BYRON.

On a bright day in the summer of 1643, a light pleasure-boat shot gaily across the harbor of Boston, laden with a merry party, whose cheerful voices were long heard, mingling with the ripple of the waves, and the music of the breeze, which swelled the canvas, and bore them swiftly onward. A group of friends, who had collected on the shore to witness their departure, gradually dispersed, till, at length, a single individual only remained, whose eyes still followed the track of the vessel, though his countenance wore that abstracted air, which shewed his thoughts were detached from the passing scene. He seemed quite unconscious of the silence that succeeded this transient bustle, and a low murmur, which soon begun to spread along the shore, was equally disregarded. Suddenly a confused sound of many voices burst upon his ear, and hurried steps, as of persons in alarm and agitation, at once aroused him from his reverie. At the same moment, a hand was laid heavily on his shoulder, and a voice exclaimed, with earnestness,

"Are you insensible, Arthur Stanhope, at a moment, when every man's life is in jeopardy?"

"My father!" replied the young man, "what is the meaning of all this excitement and confusion?"

"Do you not know?" demanded the other; "a strange sail is approaching our peaceful coast; and, see! they have unfurled the standard of popish France."

"It is true, by heaven!" exclaimed young Stanhope; "and, look, father, yonder boat is flying before them; this is no time to gaze idly on; we must hasten to their rescue."

The vessel, which produced so much alarm, was, in fact, a French ship of considerable force, apparently well manned, and armed for offensive or defensive operations. The national flag streamed gaily on the wind, and, as it anchored just against Castle Island, the roll of the drum, and the shrill notes of the fife, were distinctly heard, and men were seen busied on deck, as if preparing for some important action. The little bark, already mentioned, was filled, chiefly, with females and children, bound, on an excursion of pleasure, to an island in the bay; and their terror was extreme, on thus encountering an armed vessel of the French, who had, on many occasions, shewn hostility to the colonists. The boat instantly tacked, and crowding sail, as much as prudence would permit, steered across the harbor towards Governor's Island. But it had evidently become an object of interest or curiosity to the French; their attention seemed wholly engrossed by it, and presently a boat was lowered to the water, and an officer, with several of the crew sprang into it, and rowed swiftly from the ship's side. They immediately gave chase to the pleasure-boat, which was however considerably ahead, and so ably managed, that she kept clear her distance; and with all the muscular strength, and nautical skill of the enemy, he found it impossible to gain upon her.

In the mean time, the alarm had spread, and spectators of every age, and either sex, thronged the shore, to witness this singular pursuit. The civil and military authorities prepared for defence, should it prove necessary; a battery, which protected the harbor, was hastily manned, and the militia drawn up, in rank and file, with a promptitude, not often displayed by the heroes of a train-band company. For several years, no foreign or internal enemy had disturbed the public repose, and the fortifications on Castle Island gradually fell into decay; and, from motives of economy, at this time not a single piece of artillery was mounted, or a soldier stationed there. The enemy, of course, had nothing to oppose his progress, should he choose to anchor in the inmost waters of the bay.

Governor's Island, however, at that moment, became the centre of anxiety, and every eye was fixed upon the boat, which rapidly neared the shore. The governor, as was often his custom, had on that day retired there, with his family; and, attended only by a few servants, his person was extremely insecure, should the French meditate any sinister design. In this emergency, three shallops were filled with armed men, to sail for the protection of the chief magistrate, and ascertain the intentions of the French. Young Stanhope was invested with the command of this little force; and perhaps there was no man in the colony, who would have conducted the enterprize with more boldness and address. He had entered the English navy in boyhood; and, after many years of faithful service, was rapidly acquiring rank and distinction, when the unhappy dissensions of the times threw their blighting influence on his prospects, and disappointed his well-founded hopes of still higher advancement in his profession. His

father, an inflexible Puritan, fled to New-England from the persecution of a church which he abhorred, and, with the malevolence
of narrow-minded bigotry, the heresy of the parent was punished,
by dismissing the son from that honorable station, which his
valour had attained. Deeply wounded in spirit, Arthur Stanhope
retired from the service of his country, but he carried with him, to
a distant land, the affection and esteem of his brother officers, — a
solace, which misfortune can never wrest from a noble and virtuous mind.

On the present occasion, Stanhope made his arrangements
with coolness and precision, and received from everyone, the
most prompt and zealous assistance. The alarm, which the
appearance of the French at first excited, had gradually subsided;
but still there were so many volunteers in the cause, that it was difficult to prevent the shallops from being overloaded. Constables
with their batons, and soldiers, with fixed bayonets, guarded the
place of embarkation, till, at a given signal, the boats were loosed
from their moorings, and glided gently over the waves. A loud
shout burst from the spectators, which was succeeded by a stillness so profound, that, for several moments, the measured dash of
the oars was distinctly heard on shore. An equal silence prevailed
on board the shallops, which were rowed in exact unison, while
the men, who occupied them, sat erect and motionless as automa-
tons, their fire-arms glancing in the bright sun-shine, and their
eyes occasionally turning with defiance towards the supposed
enemy.

Arthur Stanhope stood on the stern of the principal vessel,
and beside him Mr. Gibbons, a young man, who watched the
progress of the pleasure-boat with eager solicitude, — for it contained his mother and sisters. It had then nearly reached the
island; their pursuers, probably in despair of overtaking them,
had relaxed their efforts, and rested on their oars, apparently
undecided what course to follow.

"They are observing us," said Stanhope's companion,
pointing to the French, "and I doubt they will return to the protection of their ship, and scarce leave us the liberty of disputing
the way with them."

"They will consult their prudence, in doing so," replied Stanhope, "if their intentions are indeed hostile, as we have supposed."

"If!" returned the other, "why else should they give chase to
one of our peaceable boats, in that rude manner? But, thank
heaven!" he added, joyfully, "it is now safe; see! my mother has
this moment sprung on shore, with her frightened band of dam-

sels and children! ah! I think they will not *now* admire the gallant Frenchmen, as they did last summer, when La Tour's gay lieutenant was here, with his compliments and treaties!"

"I begin to think yonder vessel is from the same quarter," said Arthur, thoughtfully; "Mons. de la Tour, perhaps, wishes to renew his alliance with us, or seeks aid to carry on his quarrel with Mons. d'Aulney, his rival in the government of Acadia."

"God forbid!" said a deep, rough voice, which proceeded from the helmsman, "that we should have any fellowship with those priests of the devil, those monks and friars of popish France."

"Spoke like an oracle, my honest fellow!" said Gibbons, laughing; "it is a pity that your zeal and discernment should not be rewarded by some office of public trust."

"Truly, master Gibbons, we have fallen upon evil days, and the righteous no longer flourish, like green bay trees, in the high places of our land; but though cast out of mine honorable office, there are many who can testify to the zeal of my past services."

"I doubt not there are many who have cause to remember it," returned Gibbons, with a smile; "but bear a little to the leeward, unless you have a mind to convert yonder papists, by a few rounds of good powder and shot."

This short dialogue was broken off, by an unexpected movement of the French, who, after lingering, as in doubt, at some distance from the island, suddenly recommenced rowing towards it, and at the same time struck up a lively air on the bugle, which floated cheerily over the waves. Soon after, their keel touched the strand, close by the pleasure-boat, which was safely moored, and deserted by every individual. The principal officer then leaped on shore, and walked leisurely towards the house of governor Winthrop. Stanhope also landed in a short time, and, with Mr. Gibbons, proceeded directly to the governor's. The mansion exhibited no appearance of alarm; the windows were thrown open to admit the cooling sea breeze, children sported around the door, and cheerful voices within announced, that the stranger, who had just preceded them, was not an unwelcome guest. He was conversing apart with Mr. Winthrop, when they entered, and they instantly recognized in him, a lieutenant of M. de la Tour, who had, on a former occasion, been sent to negociate a treaty with the magistrates of Boston. He was believed to be a Hugonot, and, on that account, as well as from the personal regard which his conduct and manners inspired, he had been treated with much attention, during the time that he remained there. Mons. de Valette, —

so he was called, — had been particularly intimate with the family of Major Gibbons, a gentleman of consideration in the colony, and he quickly espied his lady in the pleasure-boat, which he discovered in the bay. Gallantly inclined to return her civilities, he endeavoured to overtake her, with the intention of inviting her aboard the ship, quite unconscious that she was flying from him in terror. But the formidable array of armed shallops, with the assemblage of people on shore, at length excited a suspicion of the truth, and he determined to follow the lady to her retreat, to explain the motives of his conduct. His apology was graciously accepted, and the late alarm became a subject of general amusement.

De Valette also improved the opportunity, to prepare governor Winthrop for the object of La Tour's voyage to Boston. M. Razilly, governor-general of the French province of Acadia, had entrusted the administration to D'Aulney de Charnisy, and St. Etienne, lord of La Tour. The former he appointed lieutenant of the western part of the colony, the latter of the eastern; they were separated by the river St. Croix. La Tour also held possession in right of a purchase, confirmed by the king's patent; and, on the death of Razilly, which happened at an early period of the settlement, he claimed the supreme command. His pretensions were violently disputed by D'Aulney; and, from that time, each had constantly sought to dispossess the other; and the most bitter enmity kept them continually at strife. Both had repeatedly endeavoured to obtain assistance from the New-England colonists; but, as yet, they had prudently declined to decide in favor of either, lest the other should prove a dangerous, or at least an annoying enemy. La Tour was, or pretended to be, a Hugonot, — which gave him a preference with the rulers of the Massachusetts; they had shewn a friendly disposition towards him, and permitted any persons, who chose, to engage in commerce with him. He had just returned from France, in a ship well laden with supplies for his fort at St. John's, and a stout crew, who were mostly protestants of Rochelle. But he found the fort besieged, and the mouth of the river shut up, by several vessels of D'Aulney's, whose force it would have been temerity to oppose. He sailed directly to Boston, to implore assistance in removing his enemy; bringing with him a commission from the king, which established his authority, as lieutenant-general in Acadia.

It was under these circumstances, that the French vessel appeared in the harbor of Boston, the innocent cause of so much alarm to the inhabitants. Governor Winthrop heard the details and arguments of De Valette, with polite attention; but he declined advancing any opinion, till he had consulted with the deputy, and other magistrates. He, however, desired Mr. Stanhope to return with the young officer to his ship, and request M. de la Tour to become a guest at the house of the chief magistrate, until his question was decided.

CHAPTER II.

Fit me with such weeds
As may beseem some well-reputed page.
                                        SHAKSPEARE.

The tardy summer of the north burst forth in all its splendor on the woods and scattered settlements of Acadia, and even the harassed garrison at St. John's, revived under its inspiriting influence. La Tour had been compelled to return to France in the autumn, for a reinforcement and supplies, leaving the fort defended only by a hireling force, which could scarcely muster fifty men, fit for active service. They were a mixture of Scotch and French, Protestants and Catholics; their personal and religious disputes kept them at continual variance; and the death of an experienced officer, who had been left in command, produced a relaxation of discipline, which threatened the most serious consequences. The protracted absence of La Tour became a subject of bitter complaint; and, as their stores, of every kind, gradually wasted away, they began to talk loudly of throwing down their arms, and abandoning their posts. In this posture of affairs, the courage and firmness of Madame la Tour alone restrained them from open mutiny. With an air of authority, which no one presumed to question, she assumed the supreme command, and established a rigid discipline, which the boldest dared not transgress. She daily witnessed their military exercises, assigned to every man his post of duty, and voluntarily submitted to the many privations which circumstances imposed on those beneath her.

M. d'Aulney, in the mean time, kept a vigilant eye on the movements of the garrison. As spring advanced, his light vessels were sent to reconnoitre as near as safety would permit; and it was evident that he meditated a decisive attack. Mad. la Tour used the utmost caution to prevent a surprise, and deceive the enemy respecting the weakness of their resources. She restricted the usual intercourse between her people, and those without the fort; and allowed no one to enter unquestioned, except a French priest, who came, at stated times, to dispense ghostly counsel to the Catholics.

On one of these occasions, as the holy father issued from a small building, which served as a chapel for his flock, he encountered the stiff figure and stern features of a Scotch Presbyterian, whom the lady of La Tour, a protestant in faith, had received into her family, in the capacity of chaplain to her household. It was on a Sabbath morning, and both had been engaged in the offices of religion with their respective congregations. Each was passing on, in silence, when the Scot suddenly stopped, directly in the other's path, and surveyed him with an expression of gloomy distrust. An indignant glow flashed across the pale features of the priest, but instantly faded away, and he stood in an attitude of profound humility, as if waiting to learn the cause of so rude an interruption. In spite of passion and prejudice, the bigoted sectary felt rebuked by the calm dignity of his countenance and manner; but he had gone too far to recede, without some explanation, and therefore sternly said,

"Our lady admits no stranger within these gates, and wo be to the wolf who climbs into the fold in sheep's clothing!"

"The priest of God," he replied, "is privileged by his holy office to administer reproof and consolation, wherever there is an ear to listen, and a heart to feel."

"The priest of Satan," muttered the other, in a low, wrathful tone, "the emissary of that wicked one, who sitteth on the seven hills, filled with all abominations."

The priest turned from him with a look of mingled pity and scorn; but his reverend opponent caught his arm, and again strictly surveying him, exclaimed,

"It is not thou, whom my lady's easy charity permits to come in hither, and lead poor deluded souls astray, with the false doctrines of thy false religion! Speak, and explain from whence thou comest, and what are thy designs?"

"Thy wrath is vain and impotent," said the priest, coolly withdrawing from his grasp; "but the precepts of my master enjoin humility, and I disdain not to answer thee, though rudely questioned. Father Ambrose hath been called to a distant province, and, by his passport I come hither, to feed the flock which he hath left."

Still dissatisfied, the chaplain was about to prosecute his interrogatories, but the singular rencontre had already collected a crowd around them, and the Catholics, with the vivacity of their country, and the zeal of their religion, began loudly to resent the insult offered the holy father. Voices rose high in altercation; but as the worthy Scot was totally ignorant of their language, he remained, for some moments, at a loss to conjecture the cause of this sudden excitement. But the menacing looks which were directed towards him, accompanied by gestures too plain to be misunderstood, at length convinced him, that he was personally interested, and he commenced a hasty retreat, when his progress was arrested by the iron grasp of a sturdy corporal, from which he found it impossible to free himself. With a countenance, in which rage and entreaty were ludicrously blended, he turned towards the priest, whose earnest expostulations were addressed, in vain, to the exasperated assailants. The corporal kept his hold tenaciously, questioning him with a volubility known only to Frenchmen, and, enraged that he was neither understood nor answered, he concluded each sentence with a shake, which jarred every sinew in the stout frame of the Scotchman. It is doubtful to what extremes the affray might have been carried, as the opposite party began to rally with equal warmth, for the rescue of their *teacher*; but, at that moment, a quick and repeated note of alarum sounded in their ears, and announced some pressing danger. Thrown into consternation by this unexpected summons, the soldiers fled confusedly, or stood stupified, and uncertain what course to pursue. Nor was their confusion diminished, when Madame la Tour appeared in the midst of them, and, with a look, which severely reproved their negligence, exclaimed,

"Why stand ye here, my gallant men, clamouring with your idle brawls, when the enemy floats before our very gates? fly to your posts, or stay and see what a woman's hand can do."

The appeal was decisive; in a moment every man filled his proper station, and throughout the fort, the breathless pause of suspense preceded the expected signal of attack or defence. M. d'Aulney had entered the river with a strong force, and owing to the negligence of the sentinels, appeared suddenly before the surprised garrison. Emboldened by meeting no resistance, he drew up his vessels against the fort, and incautiously approached within reach of the battery. Perceiving his error too late, he immediately tacked, and gave a signal to bear off, which was promptly obeyed by the lighter vessels. But before his own, which was more unwieldly, could escape, Madame la Tour seized the favourable moment, and, with her own hand, discharged a piece of artillery, which so materially damaged the vessel, that it was found difficult to remove her from the incessant fire, which was then opened upon her. It was, however, effected; but, though repulsed at that time, it was not probable that D'Aulney would relinquish his designs; and, apprehensive that he might attempt a landing below the fort, a double guard was set, and every precaution taken to prevent another surprise.

Madame la Tour, till the last moment of danger, was every where conspicuous, dispensing her orders with the cool presence of mind, which would have honored a veteran commander. It was near the close of day, when she retired from the presence of the garrison, to seek repose from her arduous duties. In passing an angle of the fort, she was attracted by the sound of light footsteps; and, as she paused an instant, a figure bounded from the shadow of the wall, and stood before her, wrapped in a military cloak, which completely enveloped its person.

"Who are you?" demanded Madame de la Tour.

"I am ashamed to tell you," replied a soft, sweet voice, which the lady instantly recognized; "but if you can forgive me, I will uncover myself, for, indeed, I am well nigh suffocated already."

"Foolish child! where have you been, and what is the meaning of all this?"

"I was coming to seek for you; but I lingered here a few moments, for, in truth, I have no fancy to approach very near those formidable guns, unless they are more peaceably disposed than they have been today, and, now I must see if you forgive my cowardice!"

With these words the cloak was hastily unloosed, and the young page of Mad. la Tour sprang lightly from its folds. A tartan kirtle, reaching below the knees, with trews of the same material, and a Highland bonnet, adorned with a tuft of eagle feathers, gave him the appearance of a Scottish youth; — but the sparkling black eyes, the clear brunette complexion, and the jetty locks which clustered around its brow and neck, proclaimed him the native of a warmer and brighter climate. Half laughing, yet blushing with shame, the boy looked with arch timidity in his lady's face, as if deprecating the expected reproof; but she smiled affectionately on him, and said,

"I have nothing to forgive, my child; God knows this is but a poor place for one so young and delicate as you, and I wonder not, that your courage is sometimes tested beyond its strength. I would not wish you to share the dangers which it is my duty to encounter."

"I should fear nothing could I really be of service to you," replied the page, "but, today, for instance, I must have been sadly in your way, and I am very sure the first cannon ball would have carried me off the walls."

"The enemy would doubtless aim at so important a mark," said the lady, smiling, "but go now, — your valour will never win the spurs of knighthood."

"I am not ambitious of such an honour," he answered gaily; "you know I am but a fair-weather sort of page, fit only to hover around my lady's bower, in the season of flowers and sunshine."

"Mine is no bower of ease," said Mad. la Tour; "but with all its perils, I am resolved to guard it with my life, and resign it only into the hands of my lord. You have promised to assist me," she added, after a moment's pause, "and I wish you to redeem your word by remaining here till I return. I care not to trust the faith of those idle soldiers, who, perchance, think they have done enough of duty today, and your keener eyes may keep a closer watch on the landing place, and sooner espy the motions of the enemy, who still hold their station below."

"This I can do with pleasure," said the page, "and I am as brave as heart can wish, when there is no danger nigh. I love to linger under the open sky in the twilight of these bright days, which are so cheering after the damp fogs of spring, that I can hardly regret the eternal sunshine of my own dear France."

"Well, do not forget my commission in your romantic musings," replied Mad. la Tour.

The page promised obedience, and, left to himself, assumed the post of observation, retreating as far as possible from the view of the soldiers. The soft and brilliant tints of twilight slowly faded away, and the smooth surface of the river gradually darkened as its waves beat in monotonous cadence against the walls of the fort. A slight breeze, at intervals, lifted the silken folds of the banner, which drooped from the tall flag-staff, displaying the escutcheon of La Tour, surmounted by the arms of France. Far up, the noble stream, on either side, was skirted by extensive intervals, covered with the rich, bright verdure, peculiar to early summer, and occasionally rising into gentle acclivities, or terminating in impervious forests. Tufts of woodland, and large trees scattered in groups, or standing singly, like the giants of past ages, spreading their broad arms to the winds of heaven, diversified the scene; while here and there, the smoke curled gracefully from the humble cabin of the planter, and at times, the fisherman's light oar dimpled the clear waves, as he bounded homeward with the fruits of successful toil. A bright moonlight, silvering the calm and beautiful landscape, displayed the vessels of D'Aulney, riding at anchor below the fort, while a thin mist, so common in that climate, began slowly to weave around their hulks, till the tall masts and white top-sails were alone visible, floating, like a fairy fleet, in the transparent atmosphere. The page had gazed long in silent admiration, when his attention was arrested by the appearance of a human figure, gliding cautiously along beneath the parapet on which he stood. His tall, attenuated form was clothed in the loose, black garments of a monk, and the few hairs which the rules of a severe order had left on his uncovered head, were white as the snows of winter. A cowl partially concealed his features, his waist was girt by a cord of discipline, and, as he moved with noiseless steps, he seemed counting the beads of a rosary, which he carried in his hand. The page was at first on the point of speaking, believing it to be father Ambrose, the Catholic missionary; but a second glance convinced him he was mistaken, and with curiosity, mingled with a degree of awe, he leaned forward to observe him more attentively. After proceeding a few paces, he stopped, and threw back his cowl, and as he did so, his eye encountered the page, whom he surveyed strictly for a moment, then turned slowly away, and disappeared by an aperture through the outer works. The boy looked over the wall, expecting the return of this singular intruder; nor was he aware how fixedly he remained in that position, till the touch of a hand, laid lightly on his arm, recalled him to recollection. Turning quickly round, he involuntarily started back, on perceiving the object of his curiosity close beside him. His gliding footsteps and peculiar appearance awakened a transient feeling of dread; but instantly repressing it, he ventured to raise his head, and as he did so, the clear light of the moon fell full on his youthful face. The stranger was about to speak, but as the page looked towards him, the words died away on his lips, his cheeks were flushed, and his cold features glowed with sudden and strong excitement.

"Holy St. Mary, who are you?" he asked, in an accent of deep feeling, as he grasped the arm of the trembling youth.

"I am called Hector, the page of Mad. la Tour," he answered, in a voice scarce audible from terror, and shrinking from the hand which held him.

"May God forgive me!" murmured the monk to himself, as he relaxed his grasp; while, evidently by a strong effort, every trace of emotion was banished from his countenance and manner. Hector still stood before him, longing, yet afraid to flee, till the other, apparently comprehending his feelings, said, in a slow, solemn voice,

"Fear me not, boy, but go, bear this message to the lady of La Tour. Tell her, that her lord hath already spread his homeward sails, and a few hours, perhaps, will bear him hither. Tell her, that M. d'Aulney will send to parley with her for surrender; but bid her disdain his promises or threats; bid her hold out with a brave heart, and the hour of succor will surely arrive."

So saying, he turned away; and Hector hastened to the apartment of his lady.

CHAPTER III.

Herald, save thy labor;
Come thou no more for ransom, gentle herald;
SHAKSPEARE.

The arrival of some fishermen on the following morning confirmed the intelligence of father Gilbert — the name by which the
priest, who succeeded Father Ambrose, had announced himself at
the fort. They had eluded the enemy by night, and reported that
several vessels lay becalmed in the Bay of Fundy; and, though they
had not been near enough to ascertain with certainty, no doubt
was entertained, that it was the little fleet of M. la Tour, returning
with the expected supplies.

The holy character and mission of father Gilbert was his passport in every place; and, as his duty often called him to remote
parts of the settlement, and among every description of people, it
was natural that he should obtain information of passing events,
before it reached the ears of the garrison. The mysterious manner
in which he had communicated his intelligence on the preceding
evening, occasioned some surprise; but Mad. la Tour, in listening
to the relation of her page, made due allowance for the exaggerations of excited fancy; and she was also aware, that the Catholic
missionaries were fond of assuming an ambiguous air, which
inspired the lower people with reverence, and doubtless increased
their influence over them. Till within a day or two, father Gilbert
had never entered the fort; but he was well known to the poor
inhabitants without, by repeated acts of charity and kindness,
though he sedulously shunned all social intercourse, and was
remarked for the austere discipline, and rigid self-denial to which
he subjected himself.

The spirits of the garrison revived with the expectation of
relief, which was no longer considered a matter of uncertainty. In
the fulness of these renovated hopes, a boat from M. d'Aulney
approached with an officer bearing a flag of truce. He was
received with becoming courtesy, and immediately shewn into the
presence of Mad. la Tour. In spite of his contempt for female
authority, and his apathy to female charms, a feeling of respectful
admiration softened the harshness of his features, as the sturdy
veteran bent before her, with the almost forgotten gallantry of earlier years. At that period of life, when the graces of youth have just
ripened into maturity, the lady of La Tour was as highly distin-

guished by her personal attractions, as by the strength and energy of her mind. Her majestic figure displayed the utmost harmony of proportion, and the expression of her regular and striking features united, in a high degree, the sweetest sensibilities of woman, with the more bold and lofty attributes of man. At times, an air of hauteur shaded the openness of her brow, but it well became her present situation, and the singular command she had of late assumed. She received the messenger of D'Aulney with politeness, but the cold reserve of her countenance and manner, convinced him, that his task was difficult, if not hopeless. For an instant, his experienced eye drooped beneath her piercing glance; and, perceiving her advantage, she was the first to break the silence.

"What message from my lord of D'Aulney," she asked, "procures me the honor of this interview? or is it too bold for a woman's ear, that you remain thus silent? I have but brief time to spend in words, and would quickly learn what brave service he now demands of me?"

"My lord of D'Aulney," replied the officer, "bids me tell you, that he wars not with women; that he respects your weakness, and forgives the injuries which you have sought to do him."

"Forgives!" said the lady, with a contemptuous smile; "thy lord is gracious and merciful, — aye, merciful to himself, perhaps, and careful for his poor vessels, which but yesterday shivered beneath our cannon! Is this all?"

"He requires of you," resumed the officer, piqued by her scornful manner, "the restoration of those rights, which the lord of la Tour hath unjustly usurped; he requires the submission of this garrison, and the possession of this fort, and pledges his word, on such conditions, to preserve inviolate the life and liberty of every individual."

"Thy lord is most just and reasonable in his demands," returned the lady, sarcastically; "but hath he no threats in reserve, no terrors wherewith to enforce compliance?"

"He bids me tell you," said the excited messenger, "that if you reject his offered clemency, you do it at your peril, and the blood of the innocent will be required at your hands. He knows the weakness of your resources, and he will come with power to shake these frail walls to their foundations, and make the stoutest heart within them tremble with dismay."

"And bid him come," said the lady, every feature glowing with indignant feeling, and high resolve; "bid him come, and we will teach him to respect the rights which he has dared to infringe; to acknowledge the authority which he has presumed to insult; to withdraw the claims, which he has most arrogantly preferred. Tell him, that the lady of La Tour is resolved to sustain the honor of her absent lord, to defend his just cause to the last extremity, and preserve, inviolate, the possessions which his king hath intrusted to his keeping. Go tell your lord, that, though a woman, my heart is fearless as his own; say, that I spurn his offered mercy, I defy his threatened vengeance, and to God, the defender of the innocent, I look for succor in the hour of danger and strife."

So saying, she turned from him, with a courteous gesture, though her manner convinced him that any farther parley would be useless; and endeavoring to conceal his chagrin by an air of studied civility, the dissatisfied messenger was reconducted to the boat.

The vessels of M. d'Aulney left their anchorage below the fort, at an early hour in the morning; but it was reported, that they still lay near the mouth of the river, probably to intercept the return of La Tour. The day passed away, and he did not arrive, nor were any tidings received from him. Mad. la Tour's page remarked the unusual dejection of his lady, and, emulous perhaps of her braver spirit, resolved, if possible, to obtain some information, which might relieve her anxiety. With this intention he left the fort soon after sunset, attended only by a large Newfoundland dog, which was his constant companion, whenever he ventured beyond the gates. For some time, he walked slowly along the bank of the river, hoping to meet with some fishermen, who usually returned from their labors at the close of day, and were most likely to have gathered the tidings which he wished to learn. The gloom of evening, which had deepened around him, was gradually dispersed by the light of the rising moon; and as he stood alone in that solitary place, the recollection of his interview with the strange priest on the preceding evening, recurred to his imagination with a pertinacity, which he vainly endeavored to resist. He looked carefully round, almost expecting to see the tall, ghostlike figure of the holy father again beside him; but there was no sound abroad, except the sighing of the wind and waves; and the shadows of the trees lay unbroken on the velvet turf. From this disquiet musing, so foreign to his light and careless disposition, the page was at length agreeably roused by the quick dash of oars, and in a moment he perceived a small bark canoe, guided by a single individual, bounding swiftly over the waves. As it approached near the place where he stood, Hector retreated to conceal himself in a tuft of ever-greens, from whence he could, unseen, observe the person who drew near. He had reason to congratulate himself on this precaution, as the boat shortly neared the spot which he had just quitted, and in the occupant he discovered the dark features of a young Indian, who had apparently been engaged in the labor or amusement of fishing. Not caring to disclose himself to the savage, the page shrunk behind the trunk of a large pine tree, while the dog crouched quietly at his feet, equally intent on the stranger's motions, — his shaggy ears bent to the ground, and his intelligent eyes turned often inquiringly to his master's face, as if to consult his wishes and inclination.

The Indian leaped from his canoe, the instant it touched the strand, and began hastily to secure it by a rope, which he fastened around the trunk of an uprooted tree. From his appearance, he belonged to one of those native tribes, who, from constant inter-course and traffic with the French Acadians, had imbibed some of the habits and ideas of civilized life. His dress was, in many respects, similar to the European's; but the embroidered mocca-sins, the cloak of deer-skins, and plume of scarlet feathers, shewed that he had not altogether abandoned the customs and finery of his own people. His figure was less tall and athletic than the generality of Indian youth, and his finely formed features were animated by an expression of vivacity and careless good-humour, very different from the usual gravity of his nation. The page looked at him with a degree of curiosity and interest which he could neither suppress nor define. Half ashamed of his own tim-idity, he resolved to address him, and seek the information he was so desirous of obtaining, if, indeed, he had been sufficiently con-versant with the French settlers to communicate his ideas in that language. While he still hesitated, the Indian had secured his canoe, and as he stooped to take something from it, he began to hum in a low voice, and presently, to the great surprise of Hector, broke into a lively French air, the words and tune of which were perfectly familiar to his ear. The dog also seemed to recognize it; he started on his feet, listened attentively, and then, with a joyful bark, sprang towards the Indian, and began to fawn around him and lick his hands, with every demonstration of sincere pleasure.

"By our lady, you are a brave fellow, my faithful Hero," said the Indian, in very pure French, as he caressed the animal; then casting a searching glance around, he continued to address him, "But how came you here, and alone, to greet your master on his return?"

The page could scarcely repress an exclamation of surprise, as he listened to the well-remembered voice; but drawing his cloak more closely round him, and confining his dark locks beneath the tartan bonnet, which he pulled over his brow, he advanced nearer, though still unseen, and said in a disguised tone,

"Methinks thou art but a sorry actor, to be thrown off thy guard by the barking of a dog; if I had a tongue so little used to keep its own counsel, I would choose a mask which it would not so readily betray."

"Thou art right, by all the saints," replied the other; "and be thou friend or foe, I will see to whom I am indebted for this sage reproof."

So saying, he darted towards the place where the page was concealed, and Hector, hiding his face as much as possible, bowed with an air of profound respect before him.

"Ha! whom have we here?" he asked, surveying the page with extreme curiosity.

"The page of my lady De la Tour;" returned Hector, his laughing eye drooping beneath the inquisitorial gaze.

"A pretty popinjay, brought out for my lady's amusement!" said the stranger, smiling; "you make rare sport with your antic tricks, at the fort yonder, I doubt not, boy."

"I am but a poor substitute for my lord's lieutenant, whose mirth was as far-famed as his courage;" returned the page, gravely.

"Thou art a saucy knave!" said the other, quickly; but instantly checking himself, he added, "and how fares it with your lady, in the absence of her lord?"

"She is well, thank heaven, but" —

"But what?" interrupted the stranger, eagerly; "is any one — has any misfortune reached her?"

"None, which she has not had the courage to resist; the baffled foe can tell you a tale of constancy and firmness, which the bravest soldier might be proud to emulate."

"Bravely spoken, my little page; and your lady doubtless found an able assistant and counsellor in you! ha! how fared it with you, when the din of battle sounded in your ears?"

"Indifferently well," said the page, with a suppressed smile; "I am but a novice in the art of war. But have you learned aught that has befallen us?"

"A rumour only has reached me, but I hope soon to obtain more accurate and satisfactory information."

"You will hardly gain admittance to the fort in that harlequin dress," said Hector; "and I can save you the trouble of attempting it, by answering all the inquiries you may wish to make."

"Can you?" asked the other, with an incredulous smile; "then you are more deeply skilled than I could think, or *wish* you to be."

"It may be so," returned the page, significantly; "but you will soon find that the knowledge which you seek to gain, is as well known to me, as to any one whom you hope to find there."

"You speak enigmas, boy," said the other, sharply; "tell me quickly to whom, and what you allude?"

"Go, ask my lady," said the page, with provoking calmness; "I may not betray the secrets of her household."

"You!" said the other, scornfully; "a pretty stripling, truly, to receive the confidence of your lady."

"If not my lady's," replied the page, "perhaps her young companion has less discretion in her choice of confidants."

"Ha!" said the stranger, starting, and changing colour, in spite of his tawny disguise; "what say you of *her*? speak; and speak truly, for I shall soon know if thou art false, from her own lips."

"*Her* lips will never contradict *my* words," returned the boy; "but go, take the pass-word, enter the fort, and see — you will not find her there."

"Not find her there?" he repeated in astonishment, and with a bewildered air; then suddenly grasping the page's arm, he said, in no gentle tone,

"Now, by my faith, boy, you test my patience beyond endurance; if I thought you were deceiving me" —

He stopped abruptly, and withdrew his hand, as a laugh, which he could no longer repress, burst from the lips of Hector, and at the same instant the heavy cloak fell from his shoulders to the ground.

"What mountebank trick is this?" demanded the stranger, angrily; but, as his eye glanced over the figure of the page, his countenance rapidly changed, and in an altered tone, he exclaimed,

"By the holy rood, you are" —

"Hush!" interrupted Hector, quickly pressing his finger on the other's lips; and, with a feeling of instinctive dread, he pointed to father Gilbert, who was approaching, and in a moment stood calmly and silently beside them. As the young man turned to scan the person of the priest, Hector hastily gathered his cloak around him, and before they were aware of his intention, fled from the spot, and was soon secure within the walls of the fort. The pretended Indian would have pursued, when he perceived the page's flight, but his steps were arrested by the nervous grasp of the priest.

"Loose your hold, sirrah!" he said, impatiently; but instantly recollecting himself, added, with a gesture of respect, "Pardon me, holy father, my mind was chafed with its own thoughts, or I should not have forgotten the reverence due to your character and office."

"Know you that boy?" asked the priest, in a tremulous voice, and without appearing to notice his apology.

"I once knew him well," returned the other, looking at the monk in surprise; "a few months since, we were companions in the fort of St. John's. But why do you question me thus?"

"Ask me not," returned the priest, resuming his habitual calmness; "but, as well might you pursue the wind, as seek to overtake that light-footed page."

"You have kept me till it is too late to make the attempt;" murmured the other; and, his thoughts reverting to what had just passed, he continued to himself, "A pretty page, truly! and who, but a fool, or a mad-cap, like myself, could have looked at those eyes once, and not know them again?"

"You are disturbed, young man," said the priest, regarding him attentively; "and that disguise, for whatever purpose assumed, seems to sit but ill upon you."

"You speak most truly, good father; but I hope to doff these tawdry garments before morning, if the saints prosper my undertaking."

"Time is waning, my son, and that which you have to do, do quickly; the dawn of day must not find you lingering here, if your safety and honor are dear to you."

"You know me!" said the young man, surprised, "but I am totally unconscious of having ever seen you before."

"I am not sought by the young and gay," replied the priest, "but we may meet again; yonder is your path," pointing towards the fort, "mine leads to retirement and solitude."

With these words he turned from him; and the young man, with hasty steps, pursued his lonely way to the fort of St. John's.

CHAPTER IV.

I am sick of these protracted
And hesitating councils:
LORD BYRON.

The appearance of M. de la Tour at Boston, became a subject of serious inquiry and discussion to the inhabitants of that place. Time had rather increased than mitigated the religious prejudices, which separated them from the parent country, and the approach of every stranger was viewed with distrust and jealousy. The restless spirit of fanaticism and faction, curbed within the narrow limits of colonial government, gladly seized on every occasion to display its blind and pertinacious zeal. The liberal temper, and impartial administration of governor Winthrop, had been often censured by the more rigid Puritans, and his open espousal of La Tour's cause, excited much discontent and animosity. Though avowedly a Hugonot, there was reason to believe La Tour embraced the sentiments of that party from motives of policy, and it was rumored that he entertained Romish priests in his fort, and permitted them to celebrate the rites of their religion. This was sufficient food for passion and prejudice; and though La Tour, and his principal officer, De Valette, were entertained with the utmost hospitality at the house of the chief magistrate, his cause obtained few advocates, and his person was, in general, regarded with suspicion and dislike. But the actions of Mr. Winthrop were always dictated by principle; he was, therefore, firm in his resolves, and the voice of censure or applause had no power to draw him from the path of duty.

La Tour had always shown himself friendly to the New-England colonists; but M. d'Aulney, who was openly a papist, had in several instances intercepted their trading vessels, and treated the crews in a most unjustifiable manner. He had also wrested a trading house, at Penobscot, from the New-Plymouth colonists, and established his own fort there, unjustly alleging, that it came within the limits of Acadia. This conduct rendered him extremely obnoxious, particularly to the inhabitants of the Massachusetts; but his vicinity to them gave him so many opportunities of annoyance, that they dreaded to increase his animosity by appearing to favor a rival. With the most discordant views, and widely differing feelings, the magistrates and deputies of Boston convened, at the governor's request, to consult on the propriety of yielding to the wishes of La Tour. A stormy council at length broke up, with the decision, that they could not, consistently with a treaty, which they had lately ratified with the neighboring provinces, render him assistance in their public capacity; neither did they feel authorized to prevent any private individuals from enlisting in his service, either on his offer of reward, or from more disinterested motives.

"We owe them thanks, even for this concession," said La Tour to his lieutenant; "and, by my faith, we will return with such a force as shall make the traitor D'Aulney fly before us to the inmost shelter of his strong hold; — aye, he may thank our clemency if we do not pursue him there, and make the foundations of his fort tremble like the walls of Jericho."

"It must be with something more than the blast of a trumpet," returned De Valette; "if common report speaks truth, he has strongly intrenched himself in this same fort that he took from the worthy puritans, some few years since. In truth, I think we do them good service by avenging this old grievance, which they have so long complained of, and I doubt if we are not indebted in some measure to this same grudge for the benefit of their assistance."

"I care not by what motives they are actuated," said La Tour, "as long as my own designs are accomplished; and our chief concern, at present, is to take advantage of this favourable crisis, and, if possible, to get under sail, before the enemy hears of our success, and makes his escape."

"Yes," said De Valette, "and before our friends have time to change their minds, and withdraw the promised assistance."

"Why do you suggest such an idea?" asked La Tour, his brow darkening with displeasure; "by heavens, they dare not provoke me by so gross an act of treachery!"

"I do not think they intend it," returned De Valette; "but you know there is a powerful opposition to our interest in this good town, and if any of their worthy *teachers* should chance to hit upon a text of scripture which they could interpret against us, — farewell to the expected aid! Nay," he added, laughing, "I believe there are already some, who fancy they see the cloven foot of popery beneath our plain exterior, and, if that should once shew itself, why, they would as soon fight for the devil, to whom they might think us very closely allied."

"You forget, Eustace," said La Tour, lowering his voice, and looking cautiously around, "that we stand on open ground, and a bird of the air may carry our secrets to some of these long-eared, canting hypocrites! but go now, muster your volunteers as soon as possible, and our sails once spread to a fair wind, their scruples will avail them little."

The apprehensions of De Valette were not without foundation, and his keen observation had detected symptoms of retraction in some who were at first most forward in their proffers of service. The decision of the magistrates had been very generally condemned by the graver part of the community; its advocates were principally found among the young and enterprising, who gladly embraced any opportunity to signalize their courage and activity. With these, Arthur Stanhope was conspicuous for his zeal and perseverance, though he had many difficulties to contend against, arising from the inveterate prejudices of his father.

"It is a cause, in which we have no lot or portion," said the elder Stanhope, in reply to his son's arguments; "neither is it right that we should draw upon ourselves the vengeance of M. d'Aulney, by strengthening the power of a rival, who, perchance, hath no more of justice, or the king's favor, than himself."

"The public," said Arthur, "is not responsible for the act of a few individuals; and the evil, if any exists, must fall entirely on our own heads."

"It is an idle distinction, which the injured party will never acknowledge," returned the father; "and I much wonder that the governor and magistrates suffer themselves to be blinded by such vain pretences."

"We shall at least serve a good cause," replied Arthur, "by humbling the arrogant pretensions of a papist, — one who has set up a cross, and openly bowed before it, on the very borders of our territory."

"And are you sure that the adventurer, La Tour, is free from the idolatry of that abominable church?" asked Mr. Stanhope.

"We should, I think, have the charity to believe so, till it is fully and fairly contradicted," said Arthur; "we know that the crew of his vessel are mostly protestants from Rochelle, and would they follow the standard of a popish adventurer?"

"You are young, Arthur," returned his father, "and know not yet the wiles of the deceiver; God forgive me, if I am uncharitable, but the testimony of many worthy persons goes to prove, that this same La Tour hath openly employed a monkish priest, dressed in the habit of a layman, as his agent in important concerns."

"These persons may have been mistaken, father; at any rate, if we do sin, it is in ignorance, and we are certainly not accountable for the errors of others."

"So, doubtless, reasoned Jehoshaphat," his father replied,

"when he was tempted, by a lying spirit, to join with Ahab, an idolater, against Ramoth-Gilead; and was he not reproved for helping the ungodly?"

"The cases appear to me widely different," said Arthur; "and, in the present instance, I think we only obey the dictates of Christian charity, which enjoins us to assist the stranger in his distress."

"You know my opinion, Arthur," returned his father, "and I shall not prohibit you from following your inclination, as you are of an age to act and judge for yourself; but I require you to weigh the matter maturely, and not yield, without due consideration, to the impulse of an adventurous disposition."

Arthur Stanhope readily promised to deliberate, and decide with the utmost caution; and the result of this deliberation was, to accept the command of a vessel of respectable force, which La Tour had taken into his service. Three, of smaller size, the whole manned by about eighty volunteers, completed the equipment. Thus successful, M. la Tour sailed from Boston, expressing the utmost respect and gratitude to its citizens, for the friendly aid they had granted to him.

The little fleet made a gallant show, spreading its white sails to woo the summer breeze, and boldly ploughing the deep waters of the bay. A parting salute rolled heavily along the adjacent shores, and was succeeded by the sprightly notes of a French horn, which floated merrily over the waves. The town, and its green environs, shortly receded, the distant hills faded in the horizon, and the emerald isles lay, like specks, on the bosom of the ocean. Soon, the blended sky and water were the only objects on which the eye could rest; and Arthur Stanhope felt his spirits rise, as he again launched forth on the changeful element which he had loved from childhood. Nothing occurred to interrupt their passage, till they had advanced far up the Bay of Fundy, when the wind suddenly died away, and left them becalmed, within a few hours sail of the St. John's. This accident was a seasonable warning to D'Aulney, who then lay near the mouth of the river, waiting for La Tour's return; but, being apprized of his reinforcement, he prudently retreated from the unequal conflict. With the caution of experience, he successfully avoided La Tour's track; and the latter, who felt already sure of his prey, had at last the vexation to discover him, at a safe distance, and when the wind and tide rendered pursuit impossible. A thick fog, which soon began to rise, entirely separated them; and approaching night rendered it expedient to anchor, until the return of day. A report of M. d'Aulney's menaced attack on the fort had already reached La Tour, though it was too confused to convey much information, or relieve his extreme anxiety. But he endured the suspense far better than his lieutenant, who made no attempt to conceal his vexation at the necessary delay. After pacing the deck for some time in silence, he suddenly exclaimed to La Tour,

"It is tedious beyond measure to lie here, becalmed almost within sight of the fort! and then so little reliance can be placed on the flying reports which we have heard! I wish, as nothing can, at any rate, be done tonight, you would allow me to push off in a boat by myself and reconnoitre with my own eyes."

"And leave me to meet the enemy without you in the morning; — is that your intention?" asked La Tour, pettishly.

"You do not ask that question seriously, I presume?" said De Valette.

"Why, not exactly, Eustace," he answered; "though I confess I think it rather a strange request to make just at this time."

"Why so?" asked De Valette; "I would only borrow a few hours from repose, and my plan may be accomplished with ease; — nor shall you have reason to complain, that I am tardy at the call of duty."

"I understand you now, my brave nephew and lieutenant," said La Tour, smiling; "you would play the lover on this moonlight night, and serenade the lady of your heart, to apprise her of your safe return."

"There was not quite so much romance in my plot," replied De Valette; "but if you permit me to execute it, I pledge myself to return before midnight; and though you are not a lover, I am sure you are far from being indifferent to the intelligence which I may bring you."

"Go, if you will, if you *can* in safety," said La Tour; "though, could your impatience brook the delay of a few short hours, it would be well — well for yourself, perhaps; for if I remember right, you could ill bear a look of coldness, and Luciè is not always lavish of her smiles."

"I fear it not," said De Valette; "she would not greet me coldly after so long an absence; and though you smile at my folly, I am not ashamed to confess my eagerness to see her."

"She already knows her power over you but too well," said La Tour; "shew her that you are indifferent — disdainful, if you like — and trust me, she will learn to prize the love, which she now pretends to slight."

"The heart of woman must be wayward indeed," said De Valette, "if such is its nature or artifice; but my hopes are not so desperate yet, and if my memory serves me truly, I have more smiles than frowns on record."

With these words, De Valette threw himself into a small boat, and in a few moments reached the shore. He entered the hut of a half civilized Indian, and to avoid being recognized by any of D'Aulney's people whom he might chance to encounter, borrowed his savage attire, and in that disguise proceeded to the fort, near which he met the page of Mad. la Tour, as has been already related.

CHAPTER V.

He that depends
Upon your favours, swims with fins of lead,
And hews down oaks with rushes. Hang ye! Trust ye?
With every minute you do change a mind.
SHAKSPEARE.

De Valette was true to his engagement, and before the promised hour, returned in safety to his ship. With the first dawn of day, the vessels were put in readiness to weigh anchor, and sail at a moment's warning. At that crisis, La Tour had the vexation of finding his plans well nigh frustrated by the stubborness of his New-England allies. Alleging that they were restricted by their engagement to see La Tour in safety to his fort, a large majority resolutely declined committing any act of aggression, or joining in an attack which might be considered beyond the limits of their treaty. Excessively provoked at what he termed their absurd scruples, La Tour sent his lieutenant to request a few of the leading men to meet aboard his vessel, hoping to prevail with them to relinquish their ill-timed doubts. He walked the quarter-deck with impatient steps, while waiting the boat's return, and even his French complaisance could not disguise the chagrin and anger which he felt.

"I have desired your attendance here, gentlemen," he said in a haughty tone, as they approached him, "to learn how far I may rely on the services which have been so freely proffered to me."

"As far as our duty to God and our country will permit, sir," replied one, whose seniority entitled him to take a lead in the discourse.

"Mr. Leveret hath spoken rightly," said another; "and I question if it is our duty to draw the sword when we are not expressly called to do so, and especially, as in this instance, when it would seem far better for it to remain in the scabbard."

"I am ignorant," said La Tour, contemptuously, "of that *duty* which would lead a man to play the coward in a moment of difficulty, and tamely turn from an enemy, who has insultingly defied him, when one effort can crush him in his grasp."

"*We* are not actuated by revenge," returned Mr. Leveret; "neither have we pledged ourselves to support your quarrel with M. d'Aulney; but touching our agreement to convoy you to your fort of St. John's, we are ready to fulfil it, even at the peril of our lives."

"These are nice distinctions," said La Tour, angrily; "and had you explained them more fully at the outset, I should have known what dependence could be placed on your protection."

"We abhor deceit," said Mr. Leveret, calmly; "and that which we have promised, we are ready to perform; but we are not permitted to turn aside from this design, to pursue an enemy who flees before us."

"As our conduct in this affair is entirely a matter of conscience and private opinion," said Arthur Stanhope, "I presume every one is at liberty to consult his own wishes, and follow the dictates of his own judgment; for myself, I have freely offered to assist M. de la Tour to the extent of my abilities, and I wait his commands in whatever service he may choose to employ me."

"I expected this, from the honour of your profession; and the frankness of your character," said La Tour, with warmth; "and believe me, your laurels will not be tarnished, in the cause you have so generously espoused."

"I trust, young man," said Mr. Leveret, "that you are aware of the responsibility you incur, by acting thus openly in opposition to the opinion of so many older and more experienced than yourself."

"I have no doubt that many will be ready to censure me," returned Stanhope; "and some, perhaps, whose judgments I much respect; but I stand acquitted to my own conscience, and am ready to give an answer for what I do, to any who have a right to question me."

"And the crew of your vessel?" — asked Mr. Leveret.

"I shall use no undue influence with any one," interrupted Stanhope; "though I think there is scarcely a man in my service, who is not resolved to follow me to the end of this enterprise."

"We part, then," said Mr. Leveret; "and may heaven prosper you in all your *lawful* undertakings."

"Your emphasis on the word *lawful*," returned Stanhope, "implies a doubt, which I hope will soon be discarded; but, in the mean time, let as many as choose return with you, and I doubt not there will be enough left with us to assist M. de la Tour on this occasion."

The conference was shortly terminated; and it was amicably settled, that those who hesitated to depart from the strict letter of their agreement, should proceed in three of the English vessels, with M. de la Tour, to fort St. John's. De Valette and Stanhope were left in command of the two largest ships, with discretionary powers to employ them as circumstances might render expedient.

The delay which these arrangements necessarily occasioned,

was improved to the utmost by M. d'Aulney. Convinced, that he was unable to cope with the superior force, which opposed him, he took advantage of a favorable wind, and, at an early hour, crowded sail for his fort at Penobscot. De Valette and Stanhope pursued, as soon as they were at liberty; but, though they had occasional glimpses of his vessels through the day, they found it impossible to come up with them. Night at length terminated the fruitless chase; they were imperfectly acquainted with the coast, and again obliged to anchor, when day-light no longer served to direct their course in the difficult waters they were navigating.

Morning shone brightly on the wild shores of the Penobscot, within whose ample basin the vessels of De Valette and Stanhope rode securely at anchor. The waves broke gently around them, and the beautiful islands, which adorn the bay, garlanded with verdure and blossoms, seemed rejoicing in the brief but brilliant summer, which had opened upon them. Dark forests of evergreens, intermingled with the lighter foliage of the oak, the maple, and other deciduous trees, covered the extensive coast, and fringed the borders of the noble Penobscot, which rolled its silver tide from the interior lakes to mingle with the waters of the ocean. The footsteps of civilized man seemed scarcely to have pressed the soil, which the hardy native had for ages enjoyed as his birthright; and the axe and ploughshare had yet rarely invaded the hunting grounds, where he pursued the wild deer, and roused the wolf from his lair. A few French settlers, who adhered to D'Aulney, had built and planted around the fort, which stood on a point of land, jutting into the broad mouth of the river, and these were the only marks of cultivation which disturbed the vast wilderness that spread around them.

The local advantages of this situation, rendered it a place of consequence, and its possession had already been severely contested. As a military post, on the verge of the English colonies, its retention was important to the French interest in Acadia; and the extensive commerce it opened with the natives in the interior, through the navigable streams, which emptied into the bay, was a source of private emolument, that D'Aulney was anxious to secure. To retain these advantages, he wished to avoid an engagement with La Tour, whose newly acquired strength rendered him, at that time, a formidable opponent. He was, therefore, anxious to preserve his small naval force from destruction, and, for that purpose, he found it necessary to run his vessels into shallow water, where the enemy's heavier ships could not follow.

This plan was accomplished during the night; and when De

Valette and Stanhope approached the fort, at an early hour, they were surprised to find that D'Aulney had drawn his men on shore, and thrown up intrenchments to defend the landing-place. Though baffled in their first design by this artifice, they were but the more zealous to effect some object which might realize the expectations of La Tour. With this intention, they passed up the narrow channel to the north of the peninsula, in boats; and landing a portion of their men, attacked M. d'Aulney in his intrenchments. The assault was so sudden and determined, that every obstacle yielded to its impetuosity, and D'Aulney in vain endeavored to rally his soldiers, who fled in confusion to the shelter of the fort, leaving several of their number dead and wounded in the trenches. Convinced, that it would be rashness to pursue, as the fort was well manned, and capable of strong resistance, the young officers drew off their men in good order, and returned to their vessels without the loss of an individual. They remained in the bay of Penobscot for several days, when, convinced that nothing more could be done at that time, they thought it advisable to return to St. John's.

Night was closing in, as the vessels drew near the entrance of the river; every sail was set, and a stiff breeze bore them swiftly onward. A bright streak still lingered in the western horizon, and in the east, a few stars began to glimmer through the hazy atmosphere. The watch-lights of the fort at length broke cheerfully on the gloom, and strongly contrasted with the dark line of forests, which frowned on the opposite shore. The boding notes of the screech-owl, and the howling of wild beasts, which came from their deep recesses, were silenced by the animating strains of martial music, which enlivened the solitary scene. They anchored before the walls, and the friendly signal of De Valette was quickly answered by the sentinel on duty. With light footsteps the young Frenchman sprang on shore, and followed by Arthur Stanhope, passed the gateway, which led to the interior of the fort.

"Methinks the garrison have retired early tonight," said De Valette; "there is scarcely a face to be seen, except a few long-favored Presbyterians; — it is a Catholic holiday, too, and our soldiers are not wont to let such pass by without a merry-making. Ho, Ronald!" he continued, addressing the guard, "what is in the wind now, my honest fellow? are you all dead, or asleep within here?"

"Neither, please your honor," he answered, in a dolorous accent; "but what is worse, they have all gone astray, and are, even now, looking with sinful eyes upon the wicked ceremonies of that abominable church of Rome."

"You are warm, good Ronald; but where is your lord?"

"Even gone with the multitude, in this evil matter; and, as our worthy teacher, Mr. Broadhead, hath observed, it is a double condemnation for one like him —"

"Hush, sirrah!" interrupted De Valette, sharply; "not a word of disrespect to your lord and commander, or I will throw you, and your worthy teacher, over the walls of the fort. Speak at once, man, and tell me, what has taken place here."

"It is a bridal, please your honor, and —"

"A bridal!" exclaimed De Valette, rapidly changing color; "and where have you found a bride and bridegroom, in this wilderness?"

"My lady's young —" Ronald began; but De Valette waited not to hear the conclusion, for at that moment a light, streaming from a low building opposite, attracted his attention, and, with nervous irritability, he advanced towards it. It was the building used for a Catholic chapel, and the light proceeded from a nuptial procession, which was then issuing from it. Two boys walked before it, in loose black garments, with white scarfs thrown over their shoulders, and bearing flaming torches in their hands. Next came father Gilbert, with slow, thoughtful steps; and La Tour beside him, with the stern, abstracted countenance of one, who had little concern in the ceremonies, which he sanctioned by his presence. Behind them was the bridegroom, a handsome young soldier, who looked fondly on the blushing girl, who leaned upon his arm, and had just plighted her faith to him, by an irrevocable vow. The domestics of La Tour's household followed, with the Catholic part of the garrison; and, as soon as the door of the chapel closed, a lively air was struck up, in honor of the joyful occasion.

"I am a fool," murmured De Valette to himself, when a full examination had satisfied him, — "an errant fool; 'tis strange, that *one* image must be forever in my mind; that I should tremble at the very sound of a bridal, lest, perchance, it might be *her's*."

Ashamed of the emotion he had involuntarily betrayed, De Valette turned to look for Stanhope, who remained on the spot, where he had left him, engrossed by a scene, which was amusing from its novelty, and the singularity of time and place where it occurred.

"You must excuse me, Stanhope," he said; "but my curiosity, for once, exceeded my politeness; it is not often that we 'marry, and give in marriage,' in this wilderness, — though I will, by and by, shew you a damsel, whom kings might sue for."

"*My* curiosity is excited now," returned Stanhope; "and, if beauty is so rare with you, beware how you lead me into temptation. It is an old remark, that love flies from the city, and is most dangerous amidst the simplicity of nature."

"Forewarned, forearmed; remember," said De Valette, laughing, "I am a true friend, but I could ill brook a rival."

CHAPTER VI.

Good my complexion! dost thou think, though
I am caparisoned like a man, I have a doublet
And hose in my disposition?
SHAKSPEARE.

De Valette and Stanhope continued to watch the procession till it stopped before the door of a comfortable house, which was occupied by La Tour and his family. There, the music ceased, the soldiers filed off to their respective quarters, and the new married pair received the parting benediction of father Gilbert. That ceremony concluded, the priest retired, as if dreading the contamination of any festive scene, attended only by the two boys who had officiated as torch-bearers, — a service generally performed in the Catholic church by young persons initiated into the holy office.

"By our lady, my good uncle," said De Valette to La Tour, who had seen, and lingered behind to speak with him, "our Puritan allies would soon withdraw their aid from us, should they chance to see, what I have witnessed this evening; — by my faith, they would think the devil was keeping a high holiday here, and that you had become his chief favorite, and prime minister."

"Your jesting is ill-timed, Eustace," returned La Tour; "you have, indeed, arrived at an unlucky hour, but we must make the best of it; and, be sure that none of the New-England men leave the ships tonight. I hope we shall not need their succors long, if you have aimed a true blow at D'Aulney. Say, where have you left him?"

"We have driven him back to his strong hold. But more of that hereafter, — Mr. Stanhope waits to speak with you."

"Mr. Stanhope is very welcome," said La Tour, advancing cordially to meet him; "and I trust no apology is necessary for the confusion in which he finds us."

"None, certainly," returned Stanhope; "and I trust you will not suffer me to cause any interruption. I am not quite so superstitious," he added, smiling, "as to fear contagion from accidentally witnessing forms, which are not altogether agreeable to my conscience."

"You deserve to be canonized for your liberality," said De Valette; "for I doubt if there could be another such rare example found, in all the New England colonies. We Hugonots," he continued, with affected gravity, "account ourselves less rigid than your self-denying sect, and are sometimes drawn into ceremonies, which our hearts abominate."

"No more of this, Eustace," said La Tour; "Mr. Stanhope must know that all of us are, at times, governed by circumstances, which we cannot control; and he has heard enough of my situation, to conceive the address which is necessary to control a garrison, composed of different nations and religions, who are often mutinous, and at all times discordant. I should scarcely at any other time have been so engaged, but Mad. de la Tour, who is really too sincere a protestant to attend a Catholic service, prevailed on me to be present at the marriage of her favorite maid, — I might almost say companion, — with a young soldier, who has long been distinguished by his fidelity in my service."

Before Stanhope could reply to this plausible explanation, their attention was attracted by the sound of approaching voices, and the sonorous tones of Mr. Broadhead, the Presbyterian minister, were instantly recognized.

"I tell thee, boy," he said, "thou art in the broad way which leadeth to destruction."

"Do you think so, father?" asked his companion, who was one of the torch-bearers, and still carried the blazing insignium of his office — "and what shall I do, to find my way out of it?"

"Abjure the devil and his works, if thou art desirous of returning to the right path," he replied.

"You mean the pope and the church, I suppose," said the boy, in a tone of simplicity; "like my lady's chaplain, who often edifies his hearers on this topic."

"It would be well for thee to hearken to him, boy; and perchance it might prove a word in season to thy soul's refreshment."

"It has sometimes proved a refreshment to my body," said the boy; "his exhortations are so ravishing, that they are apt to lull one to sound repose."

"Thou art a flippant youth!" said the chaplain, stopping abruptly, and speaking in an accent of displeasure. "But I pity thy delusion," he added, after a brief pause, "and bid thee remember, that if thou hast access to the word, and turnest from it, thou can'st not make the plea of ignorance, in extenuation of thy crime."

"It is no fault in me to believe as I have been taught," said the boy, sullenly; "and it would ill become me, to dispute the doctrines which I have received from those who have a claim on my respect and obedience."

"They are evil doctrines, child; perverse heresies to lead men astray, into the darkness of error and idolatry."

"I could not have believed it!" answered the other, gravely; "I thought I was listening to the truth, from the lips of my lady's chaplain."

"And who says, that I do not teach the truth? I, who have made it my study and delight from my youth upwards?"

"Not I, truly; but your reverence chides me for believing in error, when, my belief is daily confirmed by your own instructions and example."

"Who are you, that presumes to say so? and, with these vestments of Satan on your back, to bear witness to your falsehood?" demanded the chaplain.

"Now may the saints defend me from your anger! I did not mean to offend," said the boy, shrinking from his extended hand, and bending his head, as if to count the beads of a rosary which hung around his neck.

"Did *I* teach you this mummery?" resumed the irritated Scot; "did *I* teach you to put on those robes of the devil, and hold that lighted torch to him, as you have but now done?"

"I crave your pardon," returned the boy; "I thought it was my lady's chaplain, whom I was lighting across the yard, but your reverence knows the truth better than I do."

As he spoke, he waved the torch on high, and the light fell full upon the excited features of Mr. Broadhead. A laugh from De Valette, who had, unobserved, drawn near enough to overhear them, startled both, and checked the angry reply, which was bursting from the chaplain's lips. He surveyed the intruder a moment in stubborn silence, then quietly retreated; probably aware, from former experience, that the gay young Catholic had not much veneration for his person or character. The boy hastily extinguished his torch, murmuring, in a low voice, —

"His reverence may find his way back in the dark, as he best can; and it will be well if he does not need the light of my torch, before he is safe in his quarters: light the devil, indeed! he took good care not to think of that, till he had served his own purpose with it!"

"What are you muttering about, boy?" asked De Valette.

"About my torch, and the devil, and other good Catholics, please your honor," he answered, with a low bow.

"Have a care, sirrah!" said De Valette; "I allow no one, in my presence, to speak disrespectfully of the religion of my country."

"It is a good cloak," returned the boy; "and I would not abuse a garment, which has just been serviceable to me, however worthless it may be, in reality."

"It may have been worn by scoundrels," said De Valette; "but its intrinsic value is not diminished on that account. Would you intimate that you have assumed it to answer some sinister design?"

"And, supposing I have," he asked; "what then?"

"Why, then you are a hypocrite."

"It is well for my lord's lieutenant to speak of hypocrisy," said the boy, laughing; "it is like Satan preaching sanctity; tell the good puritans of Boston, that the French Hugonot who worshipped in their conventicle with so much decorum, is a papist, and what, think you, would they say?"

"Who are you, that dares speak to me thus?" asked De Valette, angrily.

"That is a question, which I do not choose to answer; I care not to let strangers into my secret counsels."

"You are impertinent, boy;" said De Valette, "yet your bearing shews that you have discernment enough to distinguish between right and wrong, and you must be aware that policy sometimes renders a disguise expedient, and harmless too, if neither honour or principle are compromised."

"I like a disguise, occasionally, of all things," said the boy, archly; "are you quick at detecting one?"

"Sometimes I am," returned De Valette; "but — now, by my troth," he exclaimed, starting, and gazing intently on him, "is it possible, that you have again deceived me?"

"Nothing more likely," answered the other, carelessly; "but, hush! M. de la Tour, and the stranger with him, are observing us. See! they come this way: not a word more, if you have any wish to please me."

"Stay but one moment," said De Valette, grasping his arm; "I *must* know for what purpose you are thus attired."

"Well, release me, and I will tell you the whole truth, though you might suppose it was merely some idle whim. I wished to see Annette married, and as Mad. de la Tour thought it would be out of character for her page to appear in a Catholic assembly, I prevailed on a boy, whom father Gilbert had selected to officiate in the ceremony to transfer his dress and office to me: this is all; — and now are you satisfied?"

"Better than I expected to be, I assure you; but, for the love of the saints, be careful, or this whimsical fancy of your's may lead to some unpleasant consequences."

"Never fear; I enjoy this Proteus sort of life extremely, and you may expect to see me in some new shape, before long."

"Your own shape is far better than any you can assume," said

De Valette; "and by these silken locks, which, if I had looked at, I must have known, you cannot impose on me again."

"Twice deceived, beware of the third time," said the page, laughing; and, breaking from De Valette, he was in a moment on the threshold of the door.

"Here is a newly made priest, as I live!" said La Tour, catching the page by his arm, and drawing him back a few paces. "But methinks your step is too quick and buoyant, my gentle youth, for your vocation."

The page made no reply, but drooping his head, suffered a profusion of dark ringlets to fall over his face, as if purposely to conceal his features.

"This would be a pretty veil for a girl," said La Tour, parting the hair from his forehead; "but, by my troth, these curls are out of place, on the head of a grave priest; the shaved crown would better become a disciple of the austere father Gilbert. — What, mute still, my little anchorite? Speak, if thou hast not a vow of silence on thee!"

"And if I have," said the page, pettishly, "I must break it, though it should cost me a week's penance!"

"Ha! my lady's *soi-disant* page!" exclaimed La Tour, struck by the sound of his voice, — which, in the excitement of the moment, he had not attempted to disguise, — and drawing him towards a lamp, he bent his searching eye full upon the boy's face.

"I pray you let me begone, my lady waits for me," said the page, impatiently.

"A pretty, antic trick!" continued La Tour, without regarding his entreaty, "and played off, no doubt, for some sage purpose! Look, Eustace!" he added, laughing, "but have a care, that you do not become enamoured of the holy orders!"

"Look till you are weary!" said Hector, reddening with vexation; and dashing his scarf and rosary to the ground, he hastily unfastened the collar of his long, black vest, and throwing it from him, stood before them, dressed as a page, in proud and indignant silence.

"Why, you blush like a girl, Hector," said La Tour, tauntingly; "though I think, by the flashing of your eye, it is rather from anger, than shame. Look, Mr. Stanhope, what think *you* of our gentle page, and *ci-devant* priest?"

Mr. Stanhope *was* regarding him, with an attention, which rendered him heedless of the question; he met the eye of Hector, and instantly the boy's cheeks were blanched with a deadly paleness, which was rapidly followed by a glow of the deepest crimson. An exclamation trembled on Stanhope's lips, but he forcibly repressed it, and his embarrassment was unremarked. De Valette had noticed Hector's changing complexion, and, naturally attributing it to the confusion occasioned by a stranger's presence, he took his hand with an expression of kindness, though greatly surprised to feel it tremble within his own.

"Why," asked De Valette, "are you so powerfully agitated?"

"I am not agitated," said Hector, starting as from a dream; "I was vexed, — that is all; but it is over now," and resuming his usual gaiety of manner, he turned to La Tour, and added,

"I have played my borrowed part long enough for this evening, and if your own curiosity is satisfied, and you have amused your friends sufficiently at my expense, I will again crave permission to retire."

"Go," said La Tour, — "go and doff your foolish disguises; it is, indeed, time to end this whimsical farce."

"I shall obey you," returned the page; and gladly retreated from his presence.

Fort St. John's, on that evening, presented a scene of unusual festivity. La Tour permitted his soldiers to celebrate the marriage of their comrade, and their mirth was the more exuberant, from the privations they had of late endured. Even the joy, which the return of their commander naturally inspired, had been prudently repressed, while the New-England vessels were unlading their supplies, from respect to the peculiar feelings of the people who had afforded them so much friendly assistance. These vessels had left the fort, on the morning of that day; and their departure relieved the garrison from a degree of restraint, to which they were wholly unaccustomed.

La Tour remained conversing with Arthur Stanhope, where the page, who was soon followed by De Valette, had left them, till a message from his lady requested their presence in her apartment. The scene without, was threatening to become one of noisy revel. Many of the soldiers had gathered around a huge bonfire, amusing themselves with a variety of games; and, at a little distance, a few females, their wives and daughters, were collected on a plat of grass, and dancing with the young men, to the sound of a violin. The shrill fife, the deep-toned drum, and noisy bag-pipe, occasionally swelled the concert; though the monotonous strains of the latter instrument, by which a few sturdy Scots performed their national dance, were not always in perfect unison with the gay strains of the light-hearted Frenchmen. Here and there, a gloomy Presbyterian, or stern Hugonot, was observed, stealing along at a cautious distance from these cheerful groups, on which he cast an eye of aversion and distrust, apparently afraid to venture within the circle of such unlawful pleasures.

"Keep a sharp eye on these mad fellows, Ronald," said La Tour to the sentinel on duty; "and, if there is any disturbance, let me know it, and, beshrew me, if they have another holiday to make merry with!"

"Your honor shall be obeyed," said the sentinel, in a surly tone.

"See you to it, then," continued La Tour; "and be sure that none of those English pass the gates tonight. And have a care, that you do not neglect my orders, when your own hour of merriment arrives."

"I have no lot nor portion in such things," said Ronald, gruffly; "for, as the scripture saith" —

"Have done with your texts, Ronald," interrupted La Tour; "you Scots are forever preaching, when you ought to practice; your duty is to hear and obey, and I require nothing more of you."

So saying, he turned away, leaving the guard to the solitary indulgence of his thoughts, which the amusements of that evening had disturbed, in no ordinary degree.

Mad. de la Tour, had condescended to entertain the bride and bridegroom at her own house; and permitted such of their companions as were inclined, to join them on the festive occasion. These were sufficient to form a cheerful group; apart from them, Mad. la Tour was conversing with De Valette, and a lovely girl, who seemed an object of peculiar interest to him, when La Tour entered the room with Mr. Stanhope.

"I bring you a friend, to whose services we are much indebted," said La Tour to his lady; "and I must request your assistance, in endeavoring to render this dreary place agreeable to him."

"I shall feel inclined to do all in my power, from selfish motives," returned the lady, "independently of our personal obligations to Mr. Stanhope; and, I trust, it is unnecessary to assure him, that we shall be most happy to retain him as our guest, so long as his inclination will permit him to remain."

Stanhope returned a polite answer to these civilities; but his thoughts were abstracted, and his eyes continually turned towards the young lady, whose blushing face was animated by an arch smile of peculiar meaning. La Tour observed the slight confusion of both, but, attributing it to another cause, he said,

"Allow me, Mr. Stanhope, to present you to my fair ward,

Mademoiselle de Courcy, whom, I perceive, you have already identified with the priest, and page, who acted so conspicuous a part this evening."

"My acquaintance with Mr. Stanhope is of a much longer date," she said, quickly, and rising to offer him her hand, with an air of frankness, which, however, could not disguise a certain consciousness, which sent the tell-tale blood to her cheeks.

"It has been far too long," said Stanhope, his countenance glowing with delight, "to suffer me to be deceived by a slight disguise, though nothing could be more unexpected to me, than the happiness of meeting with you here."

"My aunt looks very inquisitive," said the young lady, withdrawing her hand; and, turning to Mad. de la Tour, she continued, "I have been so fortunate as to recognize an old friend in Mr. Stanhope; one, with whose family my aunt Rossville was on terms of the strictest intimacy, during our short residence in England."

"My sister's friends are doubly welcome to me," said Mad. la Tour; "and I shall esteem the arrival of Mr. Stanhope particularly fortunate to us."

"It is singular, indeed, that you should meet so very unexpectedly, in this obscure corner of the earth!" said De Valette, endeavouring to speak with gaiety, though he had remarked their mutual embarrassment with secret uneasiness; — "how can you account for it, Luciè?"

"I am not philosophic enough to resolve such difficult questions," she answered, smiling; "but, yonder are the musicians, waiting to sooth us with the melody of sweet sounds; we are all prepared for a dance, and here is my hand, if you will look a little more in the dancing mood, — if not, I can choose another."

"Do as you like," said De Valette, carelessly; "strangers are often preferred before tried friends."

"Yes, when tried friends look coldly on us," said Luciè, "as you do now, — so, fare thee well; there is a plump damsel, with an eye like Juno's, I commend her to thee for a partner."

She turned quickly from him, and speaking a few words to Stanhope, they joined the dancers together. De Valette remained standing a few moments in moody silence; but the exhilarating strains of the violin proved as irresistible as the blast of Oberon's horn, and, selecting a pretty maiden, he mingled in the dance, and was soon again the gayest of the gay.

CHAPTER VII.

I deem'd that time, I deem'd that pride
  Had quench'd at length my boyish flame;
Nor knew, till seated by thy side,
  My heart in all, save hope, the same

LORD BYRON.

"Then you do not think Mademoiselle de Courcy very beautiful?" asked De Valette, detaining Stanhope a moment after the family had retired.

"Not exactly beautiful," replied Stanhope; "though she has, — what is in my opinion far more captivating, — grace, spirit, and intelligence, with beauty enough, I allow, to render her —"

"Quite irresistible, you would say!" interrupted De Valette; "but, in good truth, I care not to hear you finish the sentence, with such a loverlike panegyric!"

"Your admiration of her is very exclusive," said Stanhope, smiling; "but you should not ask an opinion, which you are not willing to hear candidly expressed."

"I have no fear of the truth," answered De Valette; "and, after a voluntary absence of two years, on your part, I can scarcely suspect you of feeling a very tender interest in the lady."

"Your inference is not conclusive," returned Stanhope; "and I should much doubt the truth of that love, or friendship, which could not withstand the trial of even a more prolonged absence."

"I suspect there are few who would bear that test," said De Valette, who evidently wished to penetrate the real sentiments of Stanhope; "and one must have perseverance, indeed, who can remain constant to Luciè, through all her whims and disguises."

"Her gaiety springs from a light and innocent heart," replied Stanhope; "and only renders her more piquant and interesting; — but, speaking of disguises, — how long, may I ask, has she played the pretty page, and for what purpose was the character assumed?"

"It was at the suggestion of Mad. de la Tour, I believe, and Luciè's love of frolic induced her readily to adopt it. You know the fort was seriously threatened before our return; and Mad. de la Tour, who had few around her in whom she could confide, found her little page extremely useful, in executing divers commissions, which, in her feminine attire, could not have been achieved with equal propriety."

"I do not think a fondness for disguise is natural to her," said

Stanhope; "though she seems to have supported her borrowed character with considerable address."

"Yes, she completely deceived me at first; and this evening, I again lost the use of my senses, and mistook her for the sauciest knave of a priest, that ever muttered an ave-marie."

"Long as it is, since I have seen her," said Stanhope, "I think I could have sworn to that face and voice, under any disguise."

"You obtained a full view of her features, at once," said De Valette; "when I first met her, they were carefully shaded by a tartan bonnet, and she entirely altered the tones of her voice; and this evening, again, she would scarcely have been recognized in the imperfect light, had she not suffered her vexation to betray her. But the night wanes, and it is time for us to separate; I must go abroad, and see that all things are quiet and in order, after this unusual revelling."

De Valette then quitted the house, and Stanhope gladly sought the solitude of his own apartment, where he could reflect, at leisure, on the agitating events of the few last hours. He walked to and fro, with rapid steps, till, exhausted by his excitement, he threw himself beside an open window, and endeavoured to collect the confused ideas, which crowded on his mind and memory. The noise of mirth and music had long since passed away, and the weary guard, who walked his dull round of duty in solitude and silence, was the only living object which met his eye. No sound was abroad, but the voice of the restless stream, which glittered beneath the rising moon; — the breath of midnight fanned him with its refreshing coolness, and the calm beauty of that lonely hour gradually soothed his restless spirits.

He had encountered the object of a fond and cherished attachment, but under circumstances of perplexity and doubt, which marred the pleasure of that unexpected meeting. More than two years had elapsed since he first saw Luciè de Courcy, then residing in the north of England, whither she had accompanied a maternal aunt, the widow of an Englishman of rank and fortune. Madame Rossville, who was in a declining state of health, had yielded to the importunity of her husband's connexions, and left her native land for the summer months, hoping to receive benefit from change of scene and climate. She had no children, and Luciè, whom she adopted in infancy, was dear to her, as a daughter could have been. They resided at a short distance from the elder Mr. Stanhope; and the strict Hugonot principles of the French invalid interested the rigid puritan, and led to a friendly intimacy between the families.

Arthur Stanhope had then just retired from his profession, and the chagrin and disappointment, which at first depressed his spirits, gradually yielded to the charm which led him daily to the house of Mad. Rossville. Constant intercourse and familiar acquaintance strengthened the influence, which Luciè's sweetness and vivacity had created, and he soon loved her with the fervor and purity of a young and unsophisticated heart. Yet he loved in silence, — for his future plans were frustrated, his ambitious hopes were blighted; a writ of banishment and proscription hung over his father's house, and what had he to offer to one endowed by nature and fortune with gifts, which ranked her with the proudest and noblest in the land! But love needs not the aid of words; and the sentiments of the heart, beaming in an ingenuous countenance, are more forcible than any language which the lips can utter. Luciè was too artless to disguise the feelings which she was, as yet, scarce conscious of cherishing; but Arthur read in the smile and blush which ever welcomed his approach, the sigh which seemed to regret his departure, and the eloquent expression of an eye, which varied with every emotion of her soul, a tale of tenderness as ardent and confiding as his own. The future was unheeded in the dream of present enjoyment; for who, that loves, can doubt of happiness, or bear to look forward to the melancholy train of dark and disappointed hours which time may unfold!

In the midst of these dawning hopes, Arthur Stanhope was called to a distant part of the kingdom on business, which nearly concerned his father's private interest. Lucièwept at his departure; and, for the first time, his brow was clouded in her presence, and his heart chilled by the bodings of approaching evil. Several weeks passed away, and he was still detained from home; to add to his uneasiness, no tidings from thence had reached him, since the early period of his absence. Public rumor, indeed, told him that new persecutions had gone forth against the puritans; and the inflexible temper of his father, who had long been peculiarly obnoxious to the church party, excited the utmost anxiety, and determined him, at all events, to hasten his return.

After travelling nearly through the night, Arthur ascended one of the loftiest hills in Northumberland, just as the sun was shedding his earliest radiance on a beautiful valley, which lay before him. It was his native valley, and the mansion of his father's looked cheerful amidst the group of venerable trees which surrounded it. Time, since he last quitted it, had seared the freshness of their foliage, and the golden tints of autumn had succeeded the verdure of summer. A little farther on, the house of Mad. Rossville was just discernible; and Arthur's heart bounded with transport, as he thought how soon he should again embrace those whom he most loved on earth! But a different fate awaited him, and tidings, which withered every hope he had so long and fondly cherished. The ecclesiastical tyranny, which had exiled so many of the nonconformists from their friends and country, was, at last, extended to the elder Mr. Stanhope. His estates were confiscated, and a warrant was issued for his imprisonment; but, with extreme difficulty, he succeeded in effecting an escape to the sea-coast. He was there joined by his wife; and, through the kind assistance of friends, they collected the remains of a once ample fortune, and only waited the arrival of their son, to quit their country forever, and embark for New-England.

There was yet another blow, for which Arthur was wholly unprepared. Mad. Rossville, whose health rapidly failed on the approach of cooler weather, had died a short time previous to his return, leaving her orphan niece under the protection of her only sister, who hastened to England on hearing of her danger, and arrived but a few hours before her decease. Her late cheerful abode was deserted; and Arthur could obtain no information respecting Luciè, except that she had gone back to France with her relative, immediately after the melancholy event.

"Gone, without one kind farewell, one word of remembrance!" was the first bitter reflection of Arthur, on receiving this intelligence. "She, who might have been all the world to him, whose sunny smiles could have cheered the darkest hour of affliction, — she was gone! and, amidst the attractions of wealth, and the charms of society and friends, how soon might he fade from her remembrance!"

But that was not a time to indulge the regrets of a romantic passion; the situation of his parents required the support and consolations of filial tenderness; and no selfish indulgence could, for a moment, detain him from them. He hastily abandoned the home of his childhood — the scenes of maturer happiness; and, re-passing the barrier of his native hills, in a few days rejoined his parents at the sea-port, where they waited his arrival. They had made arrangements to take passage in the first vessel which sailed for Boston, and Arthur did not hesitate a moment to attend them in their arduous undertaking. For a time, indeed, his active spirit bent beneath the pressure of disappointment, and all places were alike indifferent to him. But the excitement of new scenes and pursuits at length roused his interest, and incited him to mental exertion. With the return of spring also, hopes, which he believed forever crushed, began to regain their influence in his mind. He was about to revisit England, on some affairs of consequence; and he resolved to improve the opportunity to satisfy his anxiety respecting Luciè, and learn, if possible, what he had still left to hope or fear. But an alarming illness, which attacked his mother, and left her long in a dangerous state, obliged him to defer his design; and another winter passed away, and various circumstances still rendered the voyage impracticable. Time gradually softened, but it could not destroy, the impression of his ill-fated attachment; and, though the image of Luciè was still cherished in his remembrance, he began to regard the days of their happy intercourse as a pleasant dream which had passed away, — a delightful vision of the fancy, which he loved to contemplate, but could never hope to realise.

It was, indeed, with emotions too powerful for disguise, that he found himself again, and so unexpectedly, in the presence of his beloved Luciè. He was ignorant of the name, even, of the relative to whom Mad. Rossville had entrusted her, — he had not the most distant idea, that she was connected with the lady of La Tour; and, in approaching the fort of St. John's, he little thought, that he was so near the goal of his wishes. But the first joyful sensations were not unmingled with doubt and alarm. He found her lovely and attractive, as when he had last seen her; but, since that time, what changes had taken place, and how might her heart have altered! De Valette, young, handsome, and agreeable, confessed himself her lover; he was the favorite of her guardians, and what influence had he, or might he not obtain, over her affections!

Such reflections of mingled pain and pleasure occupied the mind of Stanhope, and alternate hopes and fears beguiled the midnight hour, and banished every idea of repose.

CHAPTER VIII.

I pray you have the ditty o'er again!
Of all the strains that mewing minstrels sing,
The lover's one for me. I could expire
To hear a man, with bristles on his chin,
Sing soft, with upturn'd eyes, and arched brows,
Which talk of trickling tears that never fall.
Let's have it o'er again.

J.S. KNOWLES.

The meditations of Stanhope were suddenly interrupted by the loud barking of a dog, which lay in his kennel below the window; and it was presently answered by a low, protracted whistle, that instantly quelled the vigilant animal's irritation. Arthur mechanically raised his head, to ascertain who was intruding on the silence of that lonely hour, and saw a figure approaching, with quick, light footsteps, which a glance assured him was M. de Valette. He was already near the building, and soon stopped beneath a window in a projecting angle, which he appeared to examine with great attention. Arthur felt a painful suspicion that this casement belonged to Luciè's apartment, and, as it was nearly opposite his own, he drew back, to avoid being observed, though he watched, with intense interest, the motions of De Valette. The young Frenchman applied a flute to his lips, and played a few notes of a lively air, — then, suddenly breaking off, he changed the measure into one so soft and plaintive, that the sounds seemed to float, like aerial harmony, upon the stillness of the night. He paused, and looked earnestly toward the window: the moon shone brightly against it, but all was quiet within, and around, while he sang, in a clear and manly voice, the following serenade:

Awake, my love! the moon on high
Shines in the deep blue, arched sky,
And through the clust'ring woodbine peeps.
To seek the couch where Lucie sleeps.

Awake, my love! for see, afar,
Shines, soft and bright, the evening star;
But oh! its brightest beams must die,
Beneath the light of Lucie's eye.

Awake, my love! dost thou not hear
The night-bird's carol, wild and clear?
But not its sweetest notes detain
When Lucie breathes her sweeter strain.

Awake, my love! the fragrant gale
Steals odours from yon spicy vale;
But can the richly perfum'd air
With Lucie's balmy breath compare?

Awake, my love! for all around,
With beauty, pleasure, hope, is crown'd
But hope nor pleasure dawn on me,
Till Lucie's graceful form I see.

Awake, my love! for in thy bower,
Thy lover spends the lonely hour; —
She hears me! — from the lattice screen
Behold my Lucie gently lean!

The window had, indeed, slowly opened, towards the conclusion of the song, and Arthur observed some one, — Luciè, he doubted not, — standing before it, partially concealed by the folds of a curtain.

"Sung like a troubadour!" exclaimed a voice, which he could not mistake; "but, prithee, my tuneful knight, were those concluding lines extempore, or had you really the vanity to anticipate the effect of your musical incantation?"

"And who but yourself, Luciè, would doubt that charms like yours could give inspiration to even the dullest muse?"

"Very fine, truly; but I will wager my life, Eustace, that mine are not the only ears, which have been charmed with this melodious ditty, — that I am not the first damsel who has reigned, the goddess of an hour, in this same serenade! Confess the truth, my good friend, and I will give thee absolution!"

"And to whom but you, my sweet Luciè, could I address such language? you, who have so long reigned sole mistress of every thought and hope of my heart!"

"Sole mistress in the wilderness, no doubt!" said the laughing girl; "where there is no other to be found, except a tawny damsel or two, who would scarcely understand your poetic flights! but you have just returned from a brighter clime, and the dark-eyed demoiselles of merry France, perchance, might thank you for such a tribute to their charms!"

"And do you think so meanly of me, Luciè," asked De Valette, reproachfully, "as to believe me capable of playing the flatterer, wherever I go, and paying court to every pretty face, that claims my admiration?"

"Nay, I think so *well* of you, Eustace; I have such an exalted opinion of your gallantry, that I cannot believe you would remain three months in the very land of glorious chivalry, and prove disloyal to the cause! Be candid, now, and tell me, if this nonpareil morceau has not served you for a passport to the favor of the pretty villagers, as you journeyed through the country?"

"I protest, Luciè, you are" —

"No protestations," interrupted Luciè, "I have not the 'faith of a grain of mustard seed,' in them; — but, in honest truth, Eustace, your muse has been wandering among the orange groves of France; she could never have gathered so much *fragrance*, and *brightness*, and all that sort of thing, from the pines and firs of this poor spot of earth!"

"And if she has culled the sweets of a milder region," said De Valette, "it is only to form a garland for one, who is worthy of the fairest flowers that blossom in the gardens of paradise."

"Very well, and quite poetic, monsieur; your Pegasus is in an ambling mood tonight; but have a care that he do not throw you, as he did, of old, the audacious mortal who attempted to soar too high. And I pray you will have more regard to the truth, in future, and not scandalize the evening star, by bringing it into your performance so out of season; it may have shone upon the vineyards of Provence, but it is long since it glittered in our northern hemisphere."

"Have you done, my gentle mentor?" asked De Valette, in an accent of vexation.

"Not quite; I wish to know whether you, or the melodious screech-owl, represent the tuneful bird of night, alluded to in the aforesaid stanzas? I have heard no other who could pour forth such exquisite notes, since my destiny brought me hither."

"And it will be long ere you hear me again," said De Valette, angrily. "I shall be careful not to excite your mirthful humor again, at my own expense!"

"Now you are not angry with me, I hope, Eustace," she said, with affected concern; "you well know, that I admire your music exceedingly; nay, I think it unrivalled, even by the choice psalmody of our worthy chaplain; and as to the poetry, I doubt if any has yet equalled it, in this our ancient settlement of St. John's."

"Farewell, Lucie," said De Valette; "when I waken you

again" —

"Oh, you did not waken me," interrupted Luciè, "I will spare your conscience that reproach; had I gone to rest, I should scarcely have risen, even had a band of fairies tuned their tiny instruments in the moonlight, beneath my window. But, go now, Eustace, — yet stay, and tell me first, if we part in charity?"

"Yes, it must be so, I suppose; I *was* vexed with you, Luciè, but you well know that your smiles are always irresistible."

"Well, you will allow that I have been very lavish of my smiles tonight, Eustace; so leave me now, lest I begin to frown, by way of variety. Adieu!"

She immediately closed the window, and De Valette turned away, playing carelessly on his flute as he retired.

"Thank heaven! he is gone;" was the mental exclamation of Stanhope, whose impatience and curiosity were painfully exercised by this protracted conversation; for he had retreated from the window, at its commencement, to avoid the possibility of hearing, what was not probably intended to reach the ears of a third person. "Would any but a favored lover," he thought, "be admitted to such an interview?" The idea was insupportable; he traversed his apartment with perturbed and hasty steps, and it was not till long after De Valette retired, that he sought the repose of his pillow, and even then, in a state of mind which completely banished slumber from his eyes.

When Stanhope looked out, on the following morning, he saw Luciè, alone in a small garden, adjoining the house, busily employed in training some flowers; and the painful impression of the last night was almost forgotten, in the impulse which he felt to join her. He was chagrined to meet De Valette, as he crossed a passage, but repressing a repugnance, which he felt might be unjustly excited, he addressed him with his usual cordiality, and they entered the garden together. Luciè's face was turned from them, and she did not seem aware of their approach, till startled by the voice of De Valette.

"You do not seem very industriously inclined," he said; "or are you resting, to indulge the luxury of a morning reverie?"

"I *was* in a most profound reverie," she replied, turning quickly round; "and you have destroyed as fair a vision, as ever dawned on the waking fancy."

"Was your vision of the past or future?" asked De Valette.

"Only of the past; I care not for the future, which is too uncertain to be trusted, and which may have nothing but misfortunes in reserve for me."

"You are in a pensive mood, just now," said De Valette; "when I last saw you, I could scarce have believed a cloud would ever cross the sunshine of your face."

"Experience might have rendered you more discerning," she answered, with a smile; "but you, who love variety so well, should not complain of the changes of my mood."

"Change, as often as you will," said De Valette; "and, in every variation, you cannot fail to please."

"And you," said Luciè, "cannot fail of seeming very foolish, till you leave off this annoying habit of turning every word into a compliment: — nay, do not look displeased," she added, gaily; "you know that you deserve reproof, occasionally, and there is no one who will administer it to you, but myself."

"But what *you* define a compliment," said Stanhope, "would probably appear, to any other person, the simple language of sincerity."

"I cannot contend against two opponents," returned Luciè; "so I may as well give up my argument, though I still maintain its validity."

"We will call it a drawn game, then," said De Valette, laughing; "so now, Luciè, candidly confess that you were disposed to find fault with me, without sufficient cause."

"There is certainly no flattery in this," replied Luciè; "but I will confess nothing, — except that I danced away my spirits last evening, and was most melodiously disturbed afterwards, by some strolling minstrel. Were you not annoyed by unseasonable music, Mr. Stanhope?"

"I heard music, at a late hour," he replied; "but it did not disturb me, as I was still awake."

As he spoke, he was vexed to feel the color mount to his very temples; and Luciè, who instantly comprehended the cause of his confusion, bent her eyes to the ground, while her cheeks were suffused with blushes. An embarrasing pause ensued; and De Valette, displeased at the secret sympathy which their looks betrayed, stooped to pluck a rose, that grew on a small bush beside him.

"What have you done, Eustace?" asked Luciè, hastily, and glad to break the awkward silence; "you have spoiled my favorite rose-bush, which I would not have given for all the flowers of the garden."

"It is a poor little thing," said De Valette, turning it carelessly in his hand; "I could gather you a dozen far more beautiful, and quite as fragrant."

"Not one that I value half as much," she answered, taking it from him, and breathing on the crushed leaves, to restore their freshness; "I have reared it with much care, from a stock which I brought from Northumberland; and it has now blossomed for the first time — a memento of many happy days."

Her words were addressed to Stanhope, and he was receiving the rose from her hand, when her countenance suddenly changed, and, closing her eyes, as if to exclude some unwelcome object, she clung to his offered arm for support. He was too much absorbed by her, to seek the cause of her alarm; but De Valette observed father Gilbert, standing at a little distance, his eyes intently fixed on Luciè, while his features betrayed the conflict of powerful emotions.

"Why are you thus agitated, Luciè?" asked De Valette, in surprise; "surely you recognize the priest; you do not fear him?"

"He *makes* me fear him, Eustace; he always looks at me so fixedly, so wildly, that I cannot — dare not meet his gaze."

"This is mere fancy, Luciè," he answered, lightly; "is it strange that even the holy father should gaze on you with earnestness?"

"It is no time to jest, Eustace," she answered, with a trembling voice; "speak to him, — he is coming hither, — I will not stay."

While she spoke, the priest drew near her, — paused a moment, — and, murmuring a few words in a low voice, turned again, and, with a thoughtful and abstracted air, walked slowly from them. De Valette followed him; and Luciè, glad to escape, returned, with Stanhope, to the house.

CHAPTER IX.

Untaught in youth my heart to tame,
My springs of life were poison'd. 'Tis too late!
Yet I am chang'd; though still enough the same
In strength, to bear what time cannot abate,
And feed on bitter fruits, without accusing fate.

LORD BYRON.

Father Gilbert stopped a few paces from the spot which Luciè had just quitted, and, leaning against a tree, appeared so entirely absorbed by his own reflections, that De Valette for some moments hesitated to address him. The rapid mutations of his countenance still betrayed a powerful mental struggle; and De Valette felt his curiosity and interest strongly awakened, by the sudden and uncontrollable excitement of one, whose usually cold and abstracted air, shewed little sympathy with the concerns of humanity. Gradually, however, his features resumed their accustomed calmness; but, on raising his eyes, and meeting the inquiring gaze of De Valette, he drooped his head, as if ashamed to have betrayed emotions, so inconsistent with the vow which professed to raise him above the influence of all worldly passions.

"I fear you are ill, father," said De Valette, approaching him with kindness; "can I do anything to assist or relieve you?"

"I *was* ill, my son," he replied; "but it is over now — passed away like a troubled phantasy, which visits the weary and restless slumberer, and flies at the approach of returning reason."

"Your language is figurative," returned De Valette, "and implies the sufferance of mental, rather than bodily pain. If such is your unhappy state, I know full well that human skill is unavailing."

"What know *you* of pain?" asked the priest, with startling energy; "*you*, who bask in the sunshine of fortune's smile, — whose days are one ceaseless round of careless gaiety, — whose repose is yet unbroken by the gnawing worm of never-dying repentance! Such, too, I was, in the spring-time of my life; I drained the cup of pleasure, — but misery and disappointment were in its dregs; I yielded to the follies and passions of my youthful heart, — and the sting of remorse and ceaseless regret have entered my inmost soul!"

"Pardon me, father," said De Valette, "if I have unconsciously awakened thoughts which time, perchance, had well nigh soothed into forgetfulness!"

"Awakened thoughts!" the priest repeated, in a melancholy voice; "they can never, never sleep! repentance cannot obliterate them, — years of penance — fastings, and vigils, and wanderings, cannot wear them from my remembrance! Look at me, my son, and may this decaying frame, which time might yet have spared, teach thee the vanity of human hopes, and lead thee to resist the impulses of passion, and to mistrust and regulate, even the virtuous inclinations of thy heart!"

"Your words will be long remembered, father!" said De Valette, touched by the sorrow of the venerable man; "and may the good saints restore peace and hope to your wounded spirit!"

"And may heaven bless you, my son, and preserve you from those fatal errors which have wrecked my peace, and withered the fairest hopes that ever blossomed on the tree of earthly happiness! Go now," he added, in a firmer tone, "forget this interview, if possible, and when we meet again, think not of what you have now heard and witnessed, but see in me only the humble missionary of the church, who, till this day" — his voice again trembled, "till *she* crossed my path" —

"*She!*" interrupted De Valette; "do you mean Mademoiselle de Courcy?"

"De Courcy!" repeated the priest, grasping the arm of Eustace, while the paleness of death overspread his features; "who bears that most unhappy name?"

"The niece of Mad. de la Tour," returned De Valette; "and, however unfortunate the name, it has, as yet, entailed no evil on its present possessor."

"Was it she, whom I just now saw with you?" asked the priest, with increasing agitation.

"It was; and pardon me, father, your vehemence has already greatly alarmed her."

"I meant it not," he replied; "but I will not meet her again — no, I dare not look again upon that face. Has she parents, young man?" he continued, after a brief pause.

"She has been an orphan from infancy," replied De Valette; "and Mad. de la Tour is almost the only relative whom she claims on earth."

"She is a protestant?" said father Gilbert, inquiringly.

"She is," said De Valette; "though her parents, I have heard, were Catholics, and Luciè has herself told me, that in her early childhood she was instructed in that faith."

"Luciè!" muttered the priest, to himself, as if unconscious of another's presence; "and *that* name too! but no, — *she* was not left among the enemies of our faith, — it is a strange — an idle dream."

He covered his face with his hands, and remained several moments, apparently in deep musing; and when he again looked up, every trace of emotion was gone, though a shade of melancholy, deeper even than usual, had settled on his features.

"Go!" he said to De Valette, "and betray not the weakness you have witnessed; go in peace, and forget, even to pity me!"

Father Gilbert's manner was too imposing to be disputed, and De Valette left him with silent reverence, — perplexed by the mystery of his words, and the singularity of his conduct. Before he reached the house, however, he had convinced himself, that the priest was not perfectly sane, and that some fancied resemblance had touched the chords of memory, and revived the fading images of early, and perhaps unhappy days. This appeared to him, the only rational way to account for his eccentricity; and under this impression, as well as from the priest's injunction, he resolved not to mention the interview and conversation to any person. He was particularly anxious to conceal it from Luciè, whose apprehensions might be increased by the account; and, in a short time, indeed, — with the lightness of an unreflecting disposition, — a circumstance which had, at the moment, so strongly impressed him, was nearly effaced from his remembrance. Father Gilbert left the fort, and its vicinity, in the course of that day; but as the priests were continually called to visit the scattered and distant settlements, his absence, though prolonged beyond the usual time, was scarcely heeded.

In the mean while, La Tour was informed that M. D'Aulney continued to embrace every opportunity to display his hostility towards him. Disappointed in the result of his meditated attack on fort St. John's, he had recourse to various petty means of injury and annoyance. The English colony, at Pemaquid, were friendly to La Tour, and their vessels frequently visited his fort to trade in the commodities of the country. A shallop from thence had put in at Penobscot, relying on the good faith of D'Aulney; but, on some slight pretence, he detained it several days, and though, at length permitted to proceed on its voyage to St. John's, the delay produced much loss and embarrassment. La Tour resolved to avenge these repeated insults; and, hearing that the fort at Penobscot was at that time weakly defended, he made immediate preparations to commence an attack on it.

Arthur Stanhope still lingered at St. John's, and every day increased his reluctance to depart from it. Happy in the society of

Luciè, he could not resolve to quit her till the hopes, which her smiles again encouraged, had received her explicit sanction or rebuke. He felt too, that honor required of him an avowal of the sentiments which he had not attempted to disguise; he, therefore, sought the earliest opportunity to reveal them, and with grateful pleasure he received from her, a blushing confession, that his affection had been long reciprocated. His happiness, however, was slightly diminished by an injunction of secresy which she imposed on him; though he found it difficult to object against the motives which induced her to urge the request. Luciè believed their attachment was already discovered; but she had no doubt that an open disclosure would occasion a prohibition from her guardian, who, during her minority, had a right to restrain her choice. She was reluctant to act in open defiance to his commands; and she also resolved never to sacrifice her happiness to his ambitious schemes. It had long been a favorite object with La Tour, to unite her to his nephew, De Valette, whose rank and expectations would have rendered an alliance equal, and, in many respects, advantageous. Mad. de la Tour also, favored the connexion; and, though Luciè had invariably discouraged their wishes, her aversion was considered as mere girlish caprice or coquetry, which would eventually yield to their solicitations and advice. De Valette's religion was the only obstacle which Mad. la Tour was willing to admit, and he possessed so many desirable qualifications, she was ready to pass that over, as a matter of minor importance. Both, she alleged, might enjoy their own opinions; and, even in so close a connexion, perfect union of religious sentiment was not essential to happiness. Luciè thought otherwise; she had been educated a protestant, and, with many of the prejudices which the persecuted Hugonots of that period could scarcely fail of cherishing towards a church which had sought to crush them by its perfidy and oppression. These feelings, alone, would have induced her to persist in a refusal; but, independently of them, she was convinced that it would never be in her power to return the affection of De Valette, with that fervor and exclusiveness which so sacred a bond demanded.

From her first acquaintance with Arthur Stanhope, Luciè had placed, perhaps, an imprudent value on his society and attentions; and when compelled during his absence to quit the scenes of their daily and happy intercourse, in haste and affliction, and without even a parting expression of kindness and regret, she felt, for a time, that her sun of happiness was shrouded in perpetual clouds. Romantic as this attachment seemed, it stood the test of time and absence, lingered in the recesses of her heart through every change of scene, and brightened the darkest shades of doubt, and difficulty, and disappointment. Hitherto, her firmness of mind and principle had enabled her to resist the wishes of her aunt, and the remonstrances of La Tour; but their importunity had, of late, increased, and evidently from an apprehension, that the undisguised partiality of Stanhope might obtain an influence over her, detrimental to their favorite and long cherished plans. Luciè sincerely regretted that her choice was so unfortunately opposed to the wishes of her aunt; and she feared to encounter the anger of La Tour, whose stern and irritable spirit, when once aroused, was uncontrollable as the stormy ocean. But time, she sanguinely believed, would remove every obstacle. Stanhope was soon to leave her, and, in his absence, she might gradually change the sentiments of Mad. la Tour; and she hoped the pride and generosity of De Valette would prompt him voluntarily to withdraw a suit, which was so unfavourably received. Even if these expectations were disappointed, she would attain her majority in the ensuing spring, when her hand would be at her own disposal, and she should no longer hesitate to bestow it, according to the dictates of her heart.

Stanhope had offered his assistance to La Tour, in the projected expedition to Penobscot; and, as the necessary arrangements were nearly completed, a few days only remained for his continuance at St. John's. To all, except Luciè, it was evident his absence would be unregretted; for he could not but remark the cold and altered manner of Mad. de la Tour, which she vainly endeavored to disguise, by an air of studied politeness; nor the reserve and petulance of De Valette, which he did not attempt to conceal. La Tour was too politic to display his dislike towards one, whose services were so useful to him; though his prejudices were, in reality, the most inveterate.

Father Gilbert returned to the fort, after an absence of three weeks, and he brought intelligence which deeply concerned La Tour. D'Aulney had entered into a negociation with the magistrates of Boston, by which he sought to engage them in his interest, to the exclusion, and evident disadvantage of La Tour. He had sent commissioners, duly authorised to conclude a treaty of peace and commerce with them, and also a letter, signed by the vice admiral of France, which confirmed his right to the government. To this was added a copy, or pretended copy, of certain proceedings, which proscribed La Tour as a rebel and a traitor. Governor Winthrop had, in vain, endeavored to heal the differences, which subsisted between the French commanders in Acadia; D'Aulney refused to accede to any conciliatory measures. Till then, the Massachusetts colony had favored La Tour, on account of his religious principles; but the authority of M. d'Aulney now seemed so well established, and his power to injure them was so extensive, that they consented to sign the articles in question. They, however, entered into no combination against La Tour, nor debarred themselves from their usual friendly intercourse with him.

M. de la Tour listened to these details with extreme indignation, and felt an increased anxiety to depart without delay. The preparations were, therefore, soon concluded, and they waited only for a favorable wind, to convey them from the fort of St. John's.

CHAPTER X.

My fear hath catch'd your fondness —

    *   *   *   *   *

Speak, is't so?
If it be so, you have wound a goodly clue;
If it be not, foreswear't: howe'er, I charge thee,
As heaven shall work in me for thine avail,
To tell me truly.
                    SHAKSPEARE.

Arthur Stanhope's protracted stay at St. John's, occasioned much discontent and repining among the crew of his vessel. Many of them became weary of their inactive life, and impatient to be restored to the friends and occupations they had left; while the laxity of the French soldiers, — the open celebration of popish ceremonies, — the very appearance of the priest, — excited the indignation of the more rigid and reflecting. The daily exhortations of Mad. de la Tour's chaplain were not calculated to allay these irritated feelings. One of the most austere of the Scotch dissenters, Mr. Broadhead, had been induced, by religious zeal, to follow the fortunes of his patron, Sir William Alexander, who, in 1621, received a grant of Acadia, or Nova Scotia, and established the first permanent settlement in that country. It had, till then, been alternately claimed and neglected, both by French and English; and he was, a few years after, induced to relinquish his grant to La Tour, whose title was confirmed by a patent from the king of England.

La Tour, in forming this settlement, was influenced principally by motives of interest; his colony was composed of adventurers from different nations, and it seemed a matter of indifference to him, to what master he owed allegiance. By the well-known treaty of St. Germain's, Acadia was ceded to the crown of France, on which it alone depended, till finally conquered by the English, when, at a much later period, its improvement and importance rendered it more worthy of serious contest. The policy of the French government, while it remained under their jurisdiction, induced them to attempt the conversion of the native tribes, as a means of advancing their own interest, and retarding the influence of the English colonies. For this purpose, they sent out Catholic missionaries, at an early period, to the different settlements; and Jesuits were particularly employed, as the address and subtlety which always distinguished that order of priests peculiarly fitted them for the difficult task of christianizing the idolatrous savages. Their power was slowly progressive; but, in time, they acquired an ascendancy, which was extended to the minutest of the secular, as well as spiritual concerns of the province.

The puritans of New-England regarded these dangerous neighbors with distrust and fear; nor could they restrain their indignation, when the emblems of the Romish church were planted on the very borders of their territory. The haughty carriage, which La Tour at first assumed, increased their aversion, and, in their weakness, rendered him justly dreaded. He prohibited the English from trading with the natives, to the east of Pemaquid, on authority from the king of France; and, when desired to shew his commission, arrogantly answered, "that his sword was sufficient, while it could overcome, and when that failed, he would find some other means to prove and defend his right." The rival, and at times, superior power of D'Aulney, however, at length reduced these lofty pretensions, till he was finally obliged to sue for the favor, which he had once affected to despise.

Mr. Broadhead, glad to escape the storms of his native country, remained through all these changes of government and religion, and, at last, found an unmolested station in the household of Mad. de la Tour. His spirit, indeed, was often vexed by La Tour's indifference towards the protestant cause, which he pretended to favor; and, even with horror, he sometimes beheld him returning from the ceremonials of the papal church. The presence of the priests, also, about the fort, was a constant annoyance to him, and he seldom encountered one of them, without a clashing of words, which, occasionally, required the interference of La Tour, or his lady. In his zeal for proselytism, he seized every opportunity to harangue the Catholic soldiers; and his wrath, at what he termed their idolatry, was commonly exhausted in indiscriminate invectives, against every ceremony and doctrine of their religion. Frequent tumults were the result of these collisions, though restrained in some measure by the commands of Mad. de la Tour, who exacted the utmost respect towards her chaplain; and La Tour, himself, found it necessary to use his authority, in preventing such dangerous excitements. He was, therefore, compelled to retire within his own immediate sphere of duty, and, however grieved and irritated by the prevalence of error around him, he in time learned to repress his feelings, at least in the presence of those, to whom they could give offence.

The arrival of a New-England vessel at St. John's, opened to Mr. Broadhead a more extensive field of labor; and he soon found many who listened with avidity to his complaints, and joined in his censures, of the conduct and principles of La Tour. His asperity was soothed by the sympathy he received from them; and without intending to injure the interests of his lord, his representations naturally weakened their confidence in him; and many began seriously to repent engaging in a cause, which they had espoused in a moment of enthusiasm, and without due consideration.

Arthur Stanhope, absorbed by one engrossing passion, had no leisure to mark the progress of this growing discontent; and his frequent absence from the vessel, which gave an appearance of alienation from their interest and concerns, increased the dissatisfaction of his people. It was, therefore, with equal surprise and displeasure, that he at length discovered their change of feeling, and received from a large majority a decided refusal to enter into any new engagements with La Tour. Their term of duty, they alleged, had already expired, — they were not satisfied with the proposed expedition, and would no longer remain in fellowship with the adherents of an idolatrous church. Anger, remonstrance, and persuasion, were equally ineffectual to change their determination. Their enlistment was voluntary, and they had already effected the object for which they engaged; they, therefore, considered themselves released from further orders, and at liberty to return to their homes; and, with a stern, yet virtuous resolution, they declared, their consciences could not be bribed by all the gold of France.

Stanhope, vexed at a result which he had so little anticipated, and conscious that he had, in reality, no control over them, for his command was merely nominal, was glad to secure the services of the few who still adhered to him, and to compromise with the remainder. With some difficulty, he prevailed on them to continue at the fort till he returned from Penobscot, consenting to abandon his vessel to their use, — for they were not willing to mingle with the garrison, — and embark himself, with as many of his own men as chose to accompany him, and a few Scots, in a smaller one of La Tour's, which could be immediately prepared for the voyage, and was better adapted to their reduced numbers.

This alteration occasioned some delay; and La Tour's impatience was, more than once, vented in imprecations on the individuals, whose sense of duty interfered with his selfish projects. An adverse wind detained them a day or two, after every arrangement was completed; but so great was La Tour's eagerness to depart, that he embarked at sun-set, on the first appearance of a favourable change, hoping to weigh anchor by the dawn of day, or sooner, should the night prove clear, and the wind shift to the desired point. Stanhope remonstrated against this haste, as his nautical experience led him to apprehend evil from it; the clouds which for some time had boded an approaching storm, indeed, seemed passing away; but dark masses still lingered in the horizon, and the turbid waters of the bay assumed that calm and sullen aspect, which so often precedes a tempest. But La Tour was obstinate in his resolution; and, as it was important that the vessels should sail in company, Stanhope yielded to his solicitations, and left the fort with that dreariness of heart, which ever attends the moment of parting from those we love.

Mad. de la Tour, soon after her husband's departure, passed the gate, on a visit of charity to a neighboring cottage. The long summer twilight was deepening on the hills, as she returned; and, with surprise, she observed Luciè loitering among a tuft of trees, which grow near the water's edge, at a short distance from her path. Believing she had come out to seek her, Mad. la Tour approached the spot where she stood; but Luciè's attention was wholly engaged by a light boat which had just pushed from the shore, and rapidly neared the vessel of Arthur Stanhope, which lay at anchor below the fort. She could not identify the only person which it contained, but a suspicion that it was Stanhope, instantly crossed her mind. Suppressing her vexation, Mad. la Tour addressed Luciè; — she started, and a crimson glow suffused her face, as she looked up and met the eyes of her aunt, fixed inquiringly on her.

"You are abroad at an unusual hour this evening, Luciè," said Mad. de la Tour, without appearing to notice her confusion.

"Yes, later than I was aware," she answered, with some hesitation; "I have been to Annette's cottage, and was accidentally detained on my return."

"Accidentally!" repeated Mad. de la Tour, with a look which again crimsoned the cheek of Luciè; "you were not detained by any ill tidings, I trust, though your tearful eyes betray emotions, which, you know, I love you too well to witness, without a wish to learn the cause."

"How can you ask the cause, dear aunt, when we have just parted from so many friends, whose absence, and probable danger, cannot but leave us anxious and dejected!"

"You were not wont to indulge a gloomy or anxious spirit,

Luciè; and why should you *now* yield to it? Nay, but an hour or two since, you parted with apparent composure from all; and what has since happened to occasion this regret? and why should you conceal it from me, who have so long been your friend and confidant?"

"From *you*, dear aunt, I would conceal nothing; you have a right to know every thought and wish of my heart; but" —

"But what?" asked Mad. la Tour, as she hesitated; "answer me one question, Luciè; has not Mr. Stanhope but just now quitted you?"

"He has," said Luciè, deeply blushing, though her ingenuous countenance told that she was relieved from a painful reserve; "and now all is known to you, — all, — and more, perhaps, than I ought, at present, to have revealed."

"More, far more, than you ought ever to have had it in your power to reveal!" said Mad. de la Tour, in an accent of displeasure; "and it is for this stranger that you have slighted the wishes of your natural guardians, — that you have rejected the love of one, in every respect worthy of your choice!"

"Those wishes were inconsistent with my duty," returned Luciè; "and that love I could never recompense! Dearest aunt," she added, and the tears again filled her eyes, "forgive me in this one instance; it is the only thought of my heart, which has been concealed from you; and, believe me, *this* was concealed, only to save yourself and me from reproaches, which, were I now mistress of my actions, I should not fear to meet."

"Rather say, Luciè, it was concealed to suit the wishes of your lover; but is it honorable in him to seek your affections clandestinely? to bind you by promises, which are unsanctioned by your friends?"

"You are unjust to him," said Luciè, eagerly; "you suspect him of a meanness, which he could never practice. I only am to blame for whatever is wrong and secret. He has never wished to disguise his attachment, and you were not slow to detect and regret it; he was encouraged by my dear aunt Rossville, but circumstances separated us, and I scarcely dared hope that we should ever meet again" —

"But you *did* meet," interrupted Mad. de la Tour, "and why all this mystery and reserve?"

"I dreaded my uncle's anger," said Luciè: "and persuaded Stanhope, against his inclination, to leave me without any explanation to my guardian, till the time arrives when I shall be at liberty to choose for myself; and till then, I have refused to enter into any engagements, — except those which my heart has long since made, and which nothing ever can dissolve."

"To me, at least, Luciè, you might have confided this; you would not have found me arbitrary or tyrannical, and methinks, the advice of an experienced friend would not have been amiss on a subject of such importance."

"I well know your lenity and affection, dear aunt," returned Luciè; "but I was most unwilling to involve you in my difficulties, and expose you to my uncle's displeasure; in time, all would have been known to you; I should have taken no important step without your advice; and why should I perplex you, with what could now be of no avail?"

"I am willing to believe you *intended* to do right, Luciè, though I am not yet convinced that you *have* done so; but we are near the gate, and will dismiss the subject till another opportunity."

Luciè gladly assented, and their walk was pursued in silence.

CHAPTER XI.

Bedimm'd
The noontide sun, called forth the mutinous winds,
And 'twixt the green sea and the azur'd vault
Set roaring war.

SHAKSPEARE.

At day-break, the vessels of La Tour and Stanhope spread their sails to a light wind, which bore them slowly from the harbor of St. John's. The fort long lingered in their view, and the richly wooded shores and fertile fields gradually receded, as the rising sun began to shed its radiance on the luxuriant landscape. But the morning, which had burst forth in brightness, was soon overcast with clouds; and the light, which had shone so cheeringly on hill and valley, like the last gleams of departing hope, became shrouded in gloom and darkness. Still, however, they kept on their course; and by degrees the wind grew stronger, and the dead calm of the sea was agitated by its increasing violence.

The confines of Acadia, which were then undefined, stretched along the borders of the bay, presenting a vast and uncultivated tract, varying through every shade of sterility and verdure; from the bare and beetling promontory, which defied the encroaching tide, the desert plain, and dark morass, to the impervious forest, the sloping upland, and the green valley, watered by its countless streams. A transient sun-beam, at times, gilded this variegated prospect, and again the flitting clouds chequered it with their dark shadows, till the dense vapor, which hung over the water, at length arose, and formed an impenetrable veil, excluding every object from the sight.

Night closed in prematurely; the ships parted company, and, in the increasing darkness, there was little prospect of joining again; nor was it possible for either to ascertain the situation of its partner. La Tour's vessel had out-sailed the other, through the day; and he had so often navigated the bay, and rivers of the coast, that every isle and headland were perfectly familiar to him. But Stanhope had little practical knowledge of its localities, and, not caring to trust implicitly to his pilot, he proceeded with the utmost caution, sounding at convenient distances, lest he should deviate from the usual course, and run aground on rocks, or in shallow water. Though with little chance of success, he caused lights to be hung out, hoping they might attract the attention of La Tour; but their rays could not penetrate the heavy mist, which concealed even the nearest objects from observation. Signal guns were also fired at intervals, but their report mingled with the sullen murmur of the wind and waves, and no answering sound was heard on the solitary deep. Apprehensive that they approached too near the land, in the gloom and uncertainty which surrounded them, Stanhope resolved to anchor, and wait for returning day.

This resolution was generally approved; for, among the adventurers who accompanied him, Stanhope could number few expert seamen, and the natural fears of the inexperienced were heightened by superstitious feelings, at that time prevalent among all classes of people. Many seemed persuaded that they were suffered to fall into danger, as a judgment for joining with papists, in a cause of doubtful equity; and they expressed a determination to relinquish all further concern in it, should they be permitted to reach the destined shore in safety. Arguments, at such a moment, were useless; and Arthur, perplexed and anxious, yet cautious to conceal his disquietude, passed the whole of that tedious night in watch upon the deck.

Another dawn revived the hopes of all, — but they were only transient; the tempest, which had been so long gathering, was ready to burst upon their heads. Clouds piled on clouds darkened the heavens, the winds blew with extreme violence, and the angry waves, crested with foamy wreaths, now bore the vessel mountain high, then sunk with a tremendous roar, threatening to engulph it in the fearful abyss. Still the ship steered bravely on her course, in defiance of the raging elements; and Stanhope hoped to guide her safely to a harbor, at no great distance, where she might ride out the storm at anchor, for destruction appeared inevitable, if they remained in the open sea. This harbor lay at an island, near the entrance of the river Schoodic, or St. Croix; and was much frequented by the trading and fishing vessels of New-England and Acadia. Already they seemed to gain the promised haven, and every eye was eagerly directed to it, with the almost certain prospect of release from danger and suspense.

It was necessary to tack, to enter the channel of the river; and, at that fatal moment, the wind struck the mainmast with a force which instantly threw it over-board; and the ship, cast on her beam-ends by the violence of the shock, lay exposed to a heavy sea, which broke over her deck and stern. The crew, roused by their immediate hazard, used every exertion to right the vessel; and Stanhope, who had not abandoned the helm since the first moment of peril, managed, with admirable dexterity, to bear her off from the dangerous shore, to which she was continually impelled by the wind and tide. But another blast, more fierce than the former, combined with the waves, to complete the work of destruction. The vessel was left a mere hulk; and the rudder, their last hope, torn away by the appalling concussion, she was driven among the breakers, which burst furiously around her.

"The ship is gone!" said Stanhope, with unnatural calmness, as he felt it reel, and on the verge of foundering; "save yourselves, if it is not too late!"

A boat had been fortunately preserved amidst the general wreck; and with the vehemence of despair, they precipitated themselves into it. It seemed perilous, indeed, to trust so frail a bark, and heavy laden as it was, amidst the boiling surge; but it was their only resource, and, with trembling anxiety, they ventured upon the dangerous experiment. Stanhope was the last to enter; and with silent, and almost breathless caution, they again steered towards the island, from which they had been so rudely driven. Some fishermen, who had found a refuge there from the storm, and witnessed the distress, which they were unable, sooner, to relieve, came to their assistance, and in a short time all were safely landed, and comfortably sheltered in huts, which had been erected by the frequenters of the island.

Stanhope's solicitude respecting La Tour was relieved by the fishermen, several of whom had seen his vessel early on that morning, standing out for Penobscot Bay; and though slightly damaged, they had no doubt she would weather the storm, which was, probably, less violent there, than in the more turbulent Bay of Fundy. Arthur was desirous of rejoining him, as soon as possible; to report his own misfortune, and assist in the execution of those plans, which had induced the voyage. But his men, in general, were still reluctant to complete their late engagement; they regarded the disaster which had so recently placed their lives in jeopardy as a signal interposition of Providence, and they resolved to obey the warning, and return to their respective homes. Stanhope, vexed with their wavering conduct, and convinced that he could not place any reliance on their services, made no attempt to detain them. The Scots, and a few of his own people, still adhered to him: and he hired a small vessel, which lay at the island, intending to proceed to Penobscot as soon as the weather would permit.

The storm continued through that day; — the evening, also, proved dark and tempestuous; but Stanhope, exhausted by fatigue, slept soundly on a rude couch, and beneath a shelter that admitted both wind and rain. He was awake, however, by the earliest dawn, and actively directing the necessary arrangements for his departure. The storm had passed away; not a cloud lingered in the azure sky, and the first tinge of orient light was calmly reflected from the waves, which curled and murmured around the beautiful island they embraced. The herbage had put on a deeper verdure, and the wild flowers of summer sent forth a richer fragrance on the fresh and balmy air. The moistened foliage of the trees displayed a thousand varying hues; and, among their branches, innumerable birds sported their brilliant plumage, and warbled their melodious notes, as if rejoicing in the restored serenity of nature.

Arthur had wandered from the scene of busy preparation; he was alone amidst this paradise of sweets, but his heart held intercourse with the loved and distant object of his hopes, whose image was ever present to his fancy. He stood against the ruins of a fort, which had been built almost forty years before, by the Sieur de Monts, who, on that spot, first planted the standard of the king of France, in Acadia. Circumstances soon after induced him to remove the settlement he had commenced there, across the bay to Port-Royal; the island was neglected by succeeding adventurers, and his labors were suffered to fall into ruin. Time had already laid his withering finger upon the walls, and left his mouldering image amid the fair creations of the youthful world. Fragments, overgrown with moss and lichen, strewed the ground; the creeping ivy wreathed its garlands around the broken walls, and lofty trees had struck their roots deep into the foundations, and threw the shadow of their branches across the crumbling pile.

The lonely and picturesque beauty of the scene, and the associations connected with it, at first diverted the current of Arthur's thoughts; but Luciè soon resumed her influence over his imagination. Yet a painful impression, that he had wasted some moments in this dream of fancy, which should have been spent in action, shortly aroused him from his musing; and, as he felt the airy vision dissolve, he almost unconsciously pronounced the name most dear to him.

That name was instantly repeated, — but so low, that he might have fancied it the tremulous echo of his own voice, but for the startling sigh which accompanied it, and struck him with almost superstitious awe. He turned to see if any one was near, and met the eyes of father Gilbert, fixed on him with a gaze of earnest, yet melancholy, enquiry. The cowl, which generally shaded his brow, was thrown back, and his cheeks, furrowed by early and habitual grief, were blanched to even unusual paleness. He grasped a crucifix in his folded hands, and his cold, stern features, were soft-ened by an expression of deep sorrow, which touched the heart of Stanhope. He bent respectfully before the holy man, but remained silent, and uncertain how to address him.

"You have been unfortunate, young man," said the priest, after a moment's pause; "but, remember that the evils of life are not inflicted without design; and happy are they, who early profit by the lessons of adversity!"

"I have escaped unharmed, and with the lives of all my com-panions," returned Stanhope; "I should, therefore, be ungrateful to rcpine at the slight evil which has befallen me; but you were more highly favored, to reach a safe harbor, before the tempest began to rage!"

"Storms and sunshine are alike to me," he answered; "for twenty years I have braved the wintry tempests, and endured the summer heats, often unsheltered in the savage desert; and still I follow, wherever the duties of my holy calling lead, imparting to others that consolation, which can never again cheer my wearied spirit. Leave me, now, young man," he added, after a brief silence; "your duty calls you hence; and why linger you here, and dream away those fleeting moments, which can never be recalled?"

"Perhaps I merit that reproof," said Stanhope, coloring highly; "but I have not been inattentive to my duty, and I am, even now, in readiness to depart."

"Pardon me, my son, if I have spoken harshly," returned the priest; "but I would urge you to hasten your departure. La Tour, ere this, has reached Penobscot; he is too rash and impetuous to delay his purpose, and one hour may turn the scale to victory or defeat."

Stanhope answered only by a gesture of respect, as he turned away from him; and he proceeded directly to the beach, where his vessel lay, reflecting, as he went along, on the singularity of father Gilbert's sudden appearance, and wondering why he should have repeated the name of Luciè, and with such evident emotion. The agitation he had betrayed, on meeting her in the garden at St. John's, was not forgotten; and Arthur had longed, yet dared not, to ask some questions which might lead to an elucidation of the seeming mystery.

The sun had scarcely risen, when Stanhope left the island of St. Croix; the wind was fair and steady, and the sea retained no traces of its recent turbulence, except some fragments of the wreck, which floated around. Their vessel was but a poor substi-tute for the one which they had lost, but it sailed well, and answered the purpose of their short voyage; and the crew were stout in heart and spirits, notwithstanding their late disasters. Stanhope particularly regretted the loss of their fire-arms and ammunition, though he had fortunately obtained a small supply from the people at the island. Early in the afternoon they entered the bay of Penobscot, and Stanhope directed his course immediately towards the fort; he ventured, at no great distance, to reconnoitre, and was surprised that he had, as yet, seen nothing of La Tour. The sun at length declined behind the western hills, leaving a flood of golden light upon the waveless deep. The extensive line of coast, indented by numerous bays, adorned with a thousand isles of every form and size, presented a rich and boundless prospect; and, graced with the charms of summer, and reposing in the calm of that glowing twilight, it seemed almost like a region of enchantment.

The serenity and beauty of such a scene was more deeply enjoyed, from the contrast which it presented to the turbulence of the preceding day; and Stanhope lingered around the coast, till warned by the gathering gloom that it was time to seek a harbor, where they might repose in security through the night. Trusting to the experience of his pilot, he entered what is called Frenchman's Bay, and anchored to the eastward of Mount Desert island. Night seemed to approach reluctantly, and gemmed with her starry train, she threw a softer veil around the lovely scenes, which had shone so brightly beneath the light of day. The wild solitudes of nature uttered no sound; the breeze had ceased its sighing, and the waves broke gently on the grassy shore. The moon rode high in the heavens, pouring her young light on sea and land; and the summit of the Blue Hills was radiant with her silver beams.

CHAPTER XII.

Mar. *I'll fight with none but thee; for I do hate thee*
      Worse than a promise-breaker.
Auf.   *We hate alike;*
      Not Afric owns a serpent, I abhor
      More than thy fame and envy.

                              SHAKSPEARE.

La Tour, in the darkness of the night succeeding his departure
from St. John's, had found it impossible to communicate with
Stanhope; and, prudently consulting his own safety in view of the
approaching storm, he crowded sail, hoping to reach some haven,
before the elements commenced their fearful conflict. In his zeal
for personal security, he persuaded himself, that Arthur's nautical
skill would extricate him from danger; but he forgot the peculiar
difficulties to which he was exposed by his ignorance of the coast,
and also, that he was embarked in a vessel far less prepared than
his own, to encounter the heavy gale which seemed mustering
from every quarter of the heavens. Perfectly familiar, himself, with
a course which he frequently traversed, — in an excellent ship,
and assisted by experienced seamen, — he was enabled to steer,
with comparative safety, through the almost tangible darkness;
and, early on the following morning, he entered the smoother
waters of Penobscot Bay, and anchored securely in one of the
numerous harbors which it embraces.

The day passed away, and brought no tidings from Stanhope;
and De Valette, though their friendship had of late been interrupted by coldness and distrust, had too much generosity to feel
insensible to his probable danger. But La Tour expressed the
utmost confidence that he had found some sheltering port, —
as the whole extent of coast abounds with harbors, which may
be entered with perfect security, — and the night proving too
tempestuous to venture abroad for intelligence, De Valette was
obliged to rest contented with hoping for the best.

La Tour wishing to obtain more minute information respecting the situation of D'Aulney, intended to proceed, first, to Pemaquid; and, should Stanhope, from any cause, fail of joining him,
he might probably receive assistance from the English at that
place, who had always been friendly to him, and were particularly
interested in suppressing the dreaded power of M. d'Aulney. But,
while busied in preparation, on the day succeeding the storm, and
repairing the slight damage which his vessel had sustained, the

report of some fishermen entirely changed the plan and destiny of the expedition. La Tour learned from them, that D'Aulney was at that time absent from his fort, having left it, two or three days before, with a small party, to go on a hunting excursion up the river Penobscot. His garrison, they added, had been recently reduced, by fitting out a vessel for France, to return with ammunition, and other supplies, in which he was extremely deficient.

This information determined La Tour to attack the fort without delay. Every thing seemed to favor his wishes, and hold out a prospect of success. Though small in numbers, he placed perfect confidence in the courage of his men, most of whom had long adhered to his service, and followed him in the desultory skirmishes in which he frequently engaged. Impetuous to a fault, and brave even to rashness, he had, as yet, been generally successful in his undertakings, and, though often unimportant, even to his own interests, they were marked by a reckless contempt of danger, calculated to inspirit and attach the followers of such an adventurer.

La Tour, piloted by a fisherman whom he took aboard, landed on a peninsula, since called Bagaduce point, on which the fort was situated. He intended to make his first attack on a farm-house of D'Aulney's, where he was told some military stores were lodged; and, from thence, bring up his men in rear of the fort. He sanguinely believed, that in the absence of the commander, it would soon yield to his sudden and impetuous assault; or, if he had been in any respect deceived, that it would be easy to secure a safe retreat to the boats from which he had landed. De Valette, in the mean time, was ordered to divert the attention of the garrison, by sailing before the walls; and, if necessary, to afford a more efficient succor.

In perfect silence, La Tour led on his little band through tangled copse-wood and impervious shades; and, with measured tread, and thoughts intent upon the coming strife, they crushed, unheeded, the wild flower which spread its simple charms before them, and burst asunder the beautiful garlands which summer had woven around their path. The melody of nature was hushed at their approach; the birds nestled in their leafy coverts; the timid hare bounded before their steps, and the squirrel looked down in silence from his airy height, as they passed on, and disturbed the solitude of the peaceful retreat.

They at length emerged from the sheltering woods, and entered an extensive plain, which had been cleared and cultivated, and, in the midst of which, stood the farm-house, already mentioned. It was several miles from the fort; a few men were stationed there, but the place was considered so secure, from its retired situation, that they were generally employed in the labors of agriculture. La Tour's party approached almost within musket shot, before the alarm was given, and the defenders had scarcely time to throw themselves into the house, and barricade the doors and windows. The besiegers commenced a violent onset, and volley succeeded volley, with a rapidity which nothing could withstand. The contest was too unequal to continue long; La Tour soon entered the house a conqueror, secured all who were in it as prisoners, and took possession of the few munitions which had been stored there. He then ordered the building to be set on fire, and the soldiers, with wanton cruelty, killed all the domestic animals which were grazing around it. Neither party sustained any loss; two or three only were wounded, and those, with the prisoners, were sent back, under a sufficient guard, to the boats; the remainder turned from the scene of destruction with utter indifference, and again proceeded towards the fort.

The noontide sun was intensely hot, and they halted a few moments on the verge of an extensive forest, to rest in its cooling shade, and allay their thirst from a limpid stream which gurgled from its green recesses. Scarcely had they resumed the line of march, when a confused sound burst upon their ears; and instantly, the heavy roll of a drum reverberated through the woods, and a party rushed on them, from its protecting shades, with overpowering force. La Tour, with a courage and presence of mind which never deserted him, presented an undaunted front to the foe, and urged his followers by encouragement and commands, to stand firm, and defend themselves to the last extremity. A few only emulated his example; the rest, seized with an unaccountable panic, sought refuge in flight, or surrendered passively to the victors.

La Tour, in vain, endeavoured to rally them; surrounded by superior numbers, and their retreat entirely intercepted, submission or destruction seemed inevitable. But his proud spirit could ill brook an alternative which he considered so disgraceful; and, left to sustain the conflict alone, he still wielded his sword with a boldness and dexterity, that surprised and distanced every opponent. Yet skill and valor united were unavailing against such fearful odds; and the weapon which he would never have voluntarily relinquished, was at length wrested from his grasp.

A smile of triumph brightened the gloomy features of M. d'Aulney, as he met the eye of his proud and defeated enemy; but La Tour returned it by a glance of haughty defiance, which fully expressed the bitterness of his chafed and unsubdued feelings. He then turned to his humbled followers, and surveyed them with a look of angry contempt, beneath which, the boldest shrunk abashed.

"Cowards!" he exclaimed, yielding to his indignation; "fear ye to meet my eye? would that its lightnings could blast ye, perjured and recreant that ye are! ay, look upon the ground, which should have drank your heart's blood before it witnessed your disgrace; look not on me, whom you have betrayed — look not on the banner of your country, which you have stained by this day's cowardice!"

A low murmur rose from the rebuked and sullen soldiers; and D'Aulney, fearing some disturbance, commanded silence, and ordered his people to prepare for instant march.

"For you, St. Etienne, lord of la Tour," he said, "it shall be my care to provide a place of security, till the pleasure of our lawful sovereign is made known concerning you."

"To that sovereign I willingly appeal," replied La Tour; "and, if a shadow of justice lingers around his throne, the rights which you have presumed to arrogate will be restored to me, and my authority established on a basis, which you will not venture to dispute."

"Let the writ of proscription be first revoked," said D'Aulney, with a sneer; "let the names of rebel, and traitor, be blotted from your escutcheon, before you appeal to that justice, or reclaim an authority which has been long since annulled."

"False, and mean-spirited!" exclaimed La Tour, scornfully; "you stoop to insult a prisoner, who is powerless in your hands, but from whose indignation you would cower, like the guilty thing you are, had I liberty and my good sword to revenge your baseness! Go, use me as you will, use me as you *dare*, M. d'Aulney, but remember the day of vengeance may ere long arrive."

"*My* day of vengeance *has* arrived," returned D'Aulney, and his eye flashed with rage; "and you will rue the hour in which you provoked my slumbering wrath."

"Your wrath has *never* slumbered," replied La Tour, "and my hatred to you will mingle with the last throb of my existence. Like an evil demon, you have followed me through life; you blighted the hopes of my youth, — the interests and ambition of my manhood have been thwarted by your machinations, and I have now no reason to look for mercy at your hands; still I defy your malice, and I bid you triumph at your peril."

"We have strong holds in that fort which you have so long

wished to possess," said D'Aulney, with provoking coolness; "and traitors, who are lodged there, have little chance of escape."

La Tour refrained from replying, even by a glance: the soldiers, at that moment, commenced their march; and guarded, with ostentatious care, he walked apart from the other prisoners towards the fort. The angry aspect of his countenance yielded to an expression of calm contempt, and through the remainder of the way he preserved an unbroken silence.

In the mean time, De Valette had strictly obeyed the instructions of La Tour. His appearance before the fort evidently excited much sensation there; and though he kept at a prudent distance, he could observe the garrison in motion, and ascertain from their various evolutions, that they were preparing for a vigorous defence. He ordered his vessel to be put in a state for action, and waited impatiently to see the standard of D'Aulney supplanted by that of De la Tour. But his illusions were dispelled by the return of a boat with the prisoners, taken at the farm-house, and a few soldiers who had escaped by flight from the fate of their companions. Vexed and mortified by a result so unexpected, De Valette hesitated what course to pursue. La Tour had not thought necessary to provide for such an exigence, as he never admitted the possibility of falling a prisoner into the hands of D'Aulney. His lieutenant, therefore, determined to sail for Pemaquid, to seek assistance, which would enable him, at least, to recover the liberty of La Tour. He also hoped to gain some information respecting Stanhope, whose services at that crisis were particularly desirable.

M. d'Aulney had returned to his fort unexpectedly on the morning of that day; and the approach of La Tour was betrayed to him by a boy, who escaped from the farm-house, at the beginning of the skirmish. Nothing could have gratified his revenge more completely, than to obtain possession of the person of his rival; and this long desired object was thus easily attained, at a moment when least expected.

The prejudices of a superior are readily embraced by those under his authority; and, as La Tour approached the fort, every eye glanced triumphantly on him, and every countenance reflected, in some degree, the vindictive feelings of the commander. But he endured their gaze with stern indifference, and his step was as firm, and his bearing as lofty, as if he entered the gates a conqueror. A small apartment, attached to the habitable buildings of the fort, which had often served on similar occasions, was prepared; for a temporary prison, until his final destination was determined. D'Aulney, himself, examined this apartment with the utmost caution, lest any aperture should be unnoticed, through which the prisoner might effect his escape. La Tour, during this research, remained guarded in an adjoining passage, and through the open door, he perceived, with a smile of scorn, what indeed seemed the superfluous care, which was taken to provide for his security. The soldiers waited at a respectful distance, awed by the courage he had displayed, and the anger which still flashed from his full dark eye.

In this interval, La Tour's attention was attracted by the sound of light footsteps advancing along the passage; and immediately a delicate female figure passed hastily on towards a flight of stairs, not far from the spot where he was standing. Her motions were evidently confused and timid, plainly evincing that she had unconsciously entered among the soldiers; and her features were concealed by a veil, which she drew closely around them. She flitted rapidly by La Tour, but at a little distance paused, in a situation which screened her from every eye but his. Throwing back her veil, she looked earnestly at him; a deep blush overspread her face, and pressing her finger on her lips, in token of silence, she swiftly descended the stairs.

That momentary glance subdued every stormy passion of his soul; early scenes of joy and sorrow rushed on his remembrance, and clasping his hands across his brow, he stood, for a time, unmindful of all around him, absorbed by his excited thoughts. But the voice of D'Aulney again sounded in his ears, and renewed the strife of bitter feelings, which had been so briefly calmed. His cheek glowed with deeper resentment, and it required a powerful effort of self-command to repress the invective that trembled on his lips, but which, he felt, it would be more than useless to indulge. He entered his prison, therefore, in silence; and, with gloomy immobility, listened to the heavy sound of the bolts, which secured the door, and consigned him to the dreariness of profound solitude.

CHAPTER XIII.

That of all things upon the earth, he hated
Your person most: that he would pawn his fortunes
To hopeless restitution, so he might
Be called your vanquisher.

SHAKSPEARE.

The first hours of misfortune are generally the most tedious; and the night which succeeded the imprisonment of La Tour appeared to him almost endless in duration. A small and closely grated window sparingly admitted the light and air of heaven; and, through its narrow openings, he watched the last beams of the moon, and saw the stars twinkle more faintly in the advancing light of morning, before he sought that repose, which entire exhaustion rendered indispensable.

He was aroused at a late hour on the following morning, from feverish slumber, by the opening of his door; and, starting up, he, with equal surprise and displeasure, recognized M. d'Aulney in the intruder. A glance of angry defiance was the only salutation which he deigned to give; but it was unnoticed by D'Aulney, who had apparently resolved to restrain the violence, which they had mutually indulged on the preceding day.

"I come to offer you freedom, M. de la Tour," he said, after a moment's hesitation, "and on terms which the most prejudiced could not but consider lenient."

"Freedom from life, then!" La Tour scornfully replied; "I can expect no other liberty, while it is in your power to hold me in bondage."

"Beware how you defy my power!" replied D'Aulney; "or provoke the wrath which may burst in vengeance on your head. You are my prisoner, De la Tour; and, as the representative of royalty here, the command of life or death is entrusted to my discretion."

"I deny that command," said La Tour, "and bid you exercise it at your peril. Prove to me the authority which constitutes you my judge; which gives you a right to scrutinize the actions of a compeer; to hold in duresse the person of a free and loyal subject of our king; — prove this, and I may submit to your judgment, I may crave the clemency, which I now despise — nay, which I would not stoop to receive from your hands."

"You speak boldly, for a rebel and a traitor!" said D'Aulney, contemptuously; "for one whose office is annulled, and whose name is branded with infamy!"

"Come you hither to insult me, false-hearted villain?" exclaimed La Tour, passionately; "prisoner and defenceless, though I now am, you may yet have cause to repent the rashness which brings you to my presence!"

"Your threats are idle," returned D'Aulney; "I never feared you, even in your greatest strength; and think you, that I can *now* be intimidated by your words?"

"What is the purport of this interview?" asked La Tour, impatiently; "and why am I compelled to endure your presence? speak, and briefly, if you have aught to ask of me; or go, and leave me to the solitude, which you have so rudely disturbed."

"I spoke to you of freedom," replied D'Aulney; "but since you persist in believing my intentions evil, it would be useless to name the terms on which I offer it."

"You can offer no terms," said La Tour, "which comport with the honor of a gentleman and a soldier to accept."

"Are you ignorant," asked D'Aulney, "that you are proscribed, that an order is issued for your arrest, and that a traitor's doom awaits you, in your native land?"

"It is a calumny, vile as your own base heart," exclaimed La Tour; "and so help me, heaven, as I shall one day prove its falsehood."

"You have been denounced at a more impartial tribunal than mine," said D'Aulney, deliberately unrolling a parchment which he carried, and pointing to the seal of France; "these characters," he added, "are traced by high authority; and need you any farther proof, that your honors are wrested from you, and your name consigned to infamy?"

"Your malice has invented this," said La Tour, glancing his eye indignantly over the contents of the scroll; "but even this shall not avail you; and, cunningly as you have woven your treacherous web around me, I shall yet escape the snare, and triumph over all your machinations!"

"It is vain to boast of deeds, which you may never be at liberty to perform," replied D'Aulney; "your escape from this prison is impossible, and, of course, your fate is entirely at my disposal. But, grossly as you have injured me, I am willing to reconcile past differences; not from any hope of personal advantage, but to preserve the peace of the colony, and sustain the honor of the government."

"That mask of disinterestedness and patriotism," said La Tour, scornfully, "is well assumed; but, beshrew me! if it does not hide some dark and selfish purpose. Reconcile!" he added, in a tone of bitterness; "that word can never pass current with us; my hatred to you is so strong, so deeply-rooted, that nothing could ever compel me to serve you, even if, by so doing, I might advance my own fortunes to the height of princely grandeur."

"Your choice is too limited to admit of dainty scruples," said D'Aulney, tauntingly; "but, you may be induced to grant from necessity, what you would refuse as a favor. You must be convinced, that your title and authority in Acadia are now abolished, and you have every reason to apprehend the severity of the law, if you are returned a prisoner to France. I offer you immediate liberty, with sufficient privileges to render you independent, on condition that you will make a legal transfer of your late government to me, and thus amicably reunite the colony, which was so unhappily divided on the death of Razilly. Put your signature to this paper, and you are that moment free."

"Now, by the holy rood!" said La Tour, bursting into a laugh of scorn; "but that I think you are jesting with me, I would trample you beneath my feet, as I do this;" and snatching the offered paper from his hand, he tore it in pieces, and stamped violently on the scattered fragments.

"You reject my proposals, then?" asked D'Aulney, pale with angry emotions.

"Dare you ask me, again, to accept them?" returned La Tour; "think you, I would sanction the slanders you have fabricated, by such a surrender of my rights? that I would thus bring reproach upon my name, and bequeath poverty and disgrace to my children?"

"It is well," replied D'Aulney; "and the consequences of your folly must fall on your own head; but, when too late, you may repent the perverseness which is driving you to destruction."

"Were the worst fate which your malevolence could devise, at this moment before me," said La Tour, "my resolution would remain unalterable. I am not so poor in spirit, as to shrink before the blast of adversity; nor am I yet destitute of followers, who will fight for my rescue, or bravely avenge my fall."

"We shall soon find other employment for them," D'Aulney coolly replied; "this fortunate expedition of yours has scattered your vaunted force, and left your fort exposed to assaults, which it is too defenceless to repel."

"Make the experiment," said La Tour, proudly; "and again you may return, vanquished by a woman's prowess. Try the valor of men, who burn to redress their master's wrongs; and, if you dare, once more encounter the dauntless courage of a wife, anxious for her husband's safety, and tenacious of her husband's honor."

"You are fortunate," said D'Aulney, sarcastically, "to possess so brave a representative; I trust, it has long since reconciled you to the chance, which prevented your alliance with one less valiant, — one, too gentle to share the fortunes of such a bold adventurer."

"Touch not upon that theme," said La Tour, starting with almost frenzied violence; "time may wear away every other remembrance, but the treachery of a friend must remain indelible and unforgiven."

"Solitude, perchance, may calm your moody feelings, and I will leave you to its soothing influence;" said D'Aulney, in a tone of assumed indifference, which was contradicted by the angry flash that darted from his eye. He laid his hand on the door, while he spoke; La Tour returned no answer, and the next moment he was left to his own reflections; and, bitter as they were, he felt that to be again alone, was a state of comparative happiness. But, whatever he endured, not a shadow of fear or apprehension obtruded on his mind. The shame of defeat, perhaps, most deeply goaded him; and his interview with D'Aulney had awakened every dark and stormy passion in his breast. Confinement was, indeed, irksome to his active spirit; but he would not admit the possibility of its long continuance; and he had no doubt, that the exertions of De Valette would soon restore him to freedom. He rightly believed, that both the pride and affection of his nephew would stimulate him to attempt it, and he hoped his efforts would be aided by Stanhope, if he had been so fortunate as to escape the storm.

Stanhope, however, was, as yet, ignorant of these events; and the morning light, which stole so heavily through the grated window of La Tour's prison-room, shone brightly on the waters of the Bay, where his vessel had anchored through the night. He was in motion at an early hour, anxious to obtain information of La Tour, though totally at a loss in what direction to seek for him. In the midst of this perplexity, he observed a boat, at some distance, slowly approaching the eastern extremity of Mount Desert island. Stanhope waited impatiently to hail the person who occupied it, believing he might receive some intelligence from him respecting La Tour. But, instead of making the nearest point of land, he suddenly tacked his boat, and bore off from the shore, apparently intending to double a narrow headland, which projected into the bay.

The little skiff moved slowly on its course, as if guided by an idle or unskilful hand, and the oars were dipped so lightly and leisurely, that they scarce dimpled the waves, or moved the boat beyond the natural motion of the tide. The earliest blush of morn was spreading along the eastern sky, and faintly tinged the surface of the deep; and, as Arthur watched the progress of the boat, his attention was arrested by the peculiar appearance of the occupant, who, on drawing near the headland, raised himself from a reclining posture, and stood erect, leaning, with one hand, on an upright oar, while he employed the other in lightly steering the boat. His tall figure, habited in the dark garments of a Romish priest, which floated loosely on the air, gave him, as he moved alone upon the solitary deep, a wild, and almost supernatural appearance. His face was continually turned towards the shore, and at times he bowed his head, and folded his hands across his breast, as if absorbed by mental devotion, or engaged in some outward service of his religion.

Arthur could not mistake the person of father Gilbert; nor was he greatly surprised at seeing him there, as he had heard much of his wandering course of life, and knew that he was in the habit of extending his pastoral visits to the remotest cabins of his flock. Stanhope thought it possible he might direct him to La Tour; and he ordered a boat to be got ready immediately, in the hope of overtaking him. But by that time, the priest had disappeared behind the projecting land, and probably proceeded on his voyage with more expedition; for when Stanhope doubled the point, he was no longer visible. Unwilling to give up the pursuit, Arthur continued on, passing through the channel between Craneberry Islands and Mount Desert, and entered a gulf which ran in on the south side of the latter. Almost at the entrance, he discovered a small boat, like the one in question, and from which he had no doubt father Gilbert had just landed.

Leaving the boatmen to wait his return, Stanhope sprang on shore without hesitation, and rapidly followed the windings of a narrow path, though ignorant where it led, and doubtful if it were trodden by wild animals, or by the foot of man. Shortly, the wood, which he traversed, terminated in an open plain, slightly elevated above the waters of the bay, that still murmured on his ear, and glanced brightly through the foliage of some trees which fringed the shore. The spot was rich in verdure, retaining marks of former cultivation, and the trees, which rose to a noble height, were evidently a succession from the earlier monarchs of the forest. Some Jesuit missionaries had taken possession of the place at an early period, planted a cross there, and called it by the name of St. Saviour. But their settlement was soon broken up by a party of English from Virginia, who claimed it for their own king, on the plea of first discovery. It was long after neglected by both nations, and the improvements, which had been commenced, were entirely neglected.

Stanhope's attention was soon arrested by the object of his search. In the midst of the plain still lay the cross, which the English had overthrown; and, close beside it, father Gilbert was kneeling, as motionless, as if life had ceased to animate him. His eyes were fastened on a crucifix, and his pale and haggard countenance wore the traces of that mental anguish, which seemed forever to pursue him. His lips were firmly closed, and every limb and feature appeared so rigid, that Arthur could scarcely repel the dreadful apprehension, that death had seized his victim alone in that solitary spot. He approached him, and was inexpressibly relieved to perceive him start at the sound of his steps, and look round, though with a vacant air, like one suddenly roused from deep and heavy sleep.

"Pardon me, if I intrude, father," said Stanhope; "but I feared you were ill, and came to ask if I could serve you."

"Who are you?" demanded the priest, wildly, and springing from his knees; "who are you, that seek me here, — here, in this spot, consecrated to remorse and sorrow?"

"It is but a few hours since I parted from you," returned Stanhope; "and had I known you purposed coming hither, I would not willingly have left you to cross the waves alone, in that frail boat."

"I know you now, young man," replied the priest, the unnatural excitement of his countenance yielding to its usual calm; "and I thank you for your care; but solitude and gloom are most congenial to me, and I endure the fellowship of men, only in compliance with the duties of my holy office. Leave me," he added; "here, at least, I would be alone."

"This is a dreary place, father" —

"Dreary!" interrupted the priest; "and it is therefore that I seek it; twenty years have passed away, since I first found refuge in its shades, from the vanities of a world which I had too long trusted; and yearly on this day, the solitary waste is witness to my remorse and penance. Be warned by this, my son; and, in thy youth, avoid the crimes and follies which lead to an old age of sorrow."

"True repentance may obliterate every sin," said Stanhope; "and why should you despair of mercy, or even of earthly happiness?"

"Happiness!" repeated the priest; "name it not to one whose headstrong passions blasted every cherished joy, and threw their withering influence on all who loved and trusted in him; mock me not with that delusive hope, which only lives in the imagination of youth and inexperience. Again I bid you leave me; this day is consecrated to active duty, and I would fortify my mind to meet its difficulties."

"Pardon me, that I trouble you with one inquiry," said Stanhope; "have you heard aught of De la Tour?"

"He is a prisoner," returned the priest; "and if you would learn more concerning him, repair, without delay, to Pemaquid, where his lieutenant waits your arrival."

Father Gilbert turned away, as he finished speaking; and Stanhope retraced his steps to the boat, musing with deep interest on the intelligence he had received. He rowed rapidly back to his vessel; and, weighing anchor, sailed for the bay of Pemaquid, impatient to rejoin De Valette, and learn the particulars of La Tour's capture.

CHAPTER XIV.

The midnight pass'd — and to the massy door,
A light step came — it paused — it moved once more;
Slow turns the grating bolt and sullen key.

LORD BYRON.

La Tour endured the first days of confinement with more patience than could have been expected from his irascible disposition; his mind was continually excited by hopes of speedy release, and plans of future vengeance. D'Aulney's visit to him was not repeated, and his solitude remained unbroken, except by the person who brought him food, and who generally performed his office in perfect silence. But the third day passed more heavily away; he listened to every sound from without his prison, and as none reached him, which announced approaching succor, he could not repress an audible expression of anger and disappointment, at his nephew's tardiness. A thousand plans of escape were formed, and instantly rejected, as visionary and impracticable. He too well knew the severe and cautious temper of D'Aulney, to suppose he would leave any avenue unguarded; and, of course, an attempt of the kind could only end in defeat, and perhaps a restriction of the few privileges he then enjoyed. A sentinel watched continually at the outside of his door; others were stationed near enough to lend assistance on a word of alarm; and his window, even if the bars could be forced, was rendered secure by the vigilance of a soldier placed beneath to protect it. His own strength and address were therefore unavailing; the conviction vexed and mortified him, and he paced his apartment with rapid steps, till his harassed feelings were wrought up to the highest pitch of irritability.

Daylight disappeared, and the evening advanced in gloom and darkness; not a star shone in the heavens, and the moon vainly struggled with the clouds which overshadowed her. A hollow blast, at intervals, swept across the grated window, then murmured into total silence; the waves rolled sullenly below, and occasionally the measured dash of oars from some passing boat was mingled with their melancholy cadence. La Tour's meditations were broken by the sentinel entering with a light; and as he placed it on a wooden stand, he lingered a moment, and regarded the prisoner with peculiar attention. He, however, took no notice of it, except to avert his face more entirely from, what he considered, a gaze of impertinent curiosity. The soldier, as he re-opened the door, again turned, and seemed on the point of speaking; but

La Tour could endure no intrusion, and a glance of angry reproof from his eye, induced a precipitate retreat. He almost instantly repented this vehemence; for that parting look was familiar to him, and possibly he might have received some desirable information.

But it was too late to recall what he had done; and La Tour again sunk into a train of reflections, though of a more tranquil nature than those which before agitated him. Recent occurrences had revived the recollections of earlier years; and he looked back, with softened feelings, on those peaceful scenes, which he had left in youth to buffet with the storms of life, and the still fiercer storms of passion. His thoughts were, at length, exclusively occupied with the appearance of the female whom he so unexpectedly encountered on the first evening of his imprisonment, and whose features he had instantly identified with an image once most dear to him; but which had, long since, been absorbed in the pursuits of interest, and the struggles of ambition. The time had indeed gone by, when associations, blended with that image, could deeply agitate him; and, connected as they were, with his aversion to D'Aulney, they tended to excite emotions of anger rather than of tenderness.

But, whatever was the nature of his feelings, they were shortly diverted to another channel by a low sound from without the door, which announced the cautious withdrawing of its bolts. The next instant it was opened by the guard who had before entered; and La Tour, surprised at his appearing so unseasonably, — for it was after midnight — was about to question him, when he pointed significantly to the door, and again hastily retired.

"Antoine!" exclaimed La Tour, suddenly recognizing in him a soldier of his own, who, on some former occasion, had been taken prisoner by D'Aulney, and voluntarily remained in his service. The call was unanswered; but presently the door again opened, and a figure entered, dressed in priestly guise, with a cowl drawn closely over his face. La Tour, at first, thought only of father Gilbert; and, with undefined expectation, rose to meet him; but another glance showed, that this person was low in stature, and altogether different in appearance from the monk. He retreated, with a sensation of keen disappointment; and believing that he saw before him some emissary from D'Aulney, he asked, impatiently,

"Who are you, that steal in upon my solitude at this untimely hour? that garb is your protection, or you might have reason to repent this rash and unwelcome intrusion!"

The object of this interrogation and menace seemed to shrink from the searching gaze of La Tour; and, without returning a word in reply, covered his face with both hands, as if still more effectually to conceal his features.

"What trick of priestcraft is this?" demanded La Tour, angrily; "is it not enough, that I am held in duresse by a villain's power, but must I be denied, even the poor privilege of bearing my confinement unmolested? What, silent yet!" he added, in a tone of sarcasm; "methinks, thou art a novice in thy cunning trade, or thou wouldst not be so chary of thy ghostly counsel, or so slow to shrive the conscience of a luckless prisoner!"

"St. Etienne!" replied a voice, which thrilled his ear, in well-remembered accents; and, at the same moment, a trembling hand removed the cowl which covered a face glowing with confusion, and confined the light ringlets, that again fell profusely around the neck and brow.

"Adèle!" exclaimed La Tour, springing towards her; then suddenly retreating to the utmost limits of the room, while every nerve shook with powerful emotion. He closed his eyes, as if fearing to look upon a face that he had last seen in the brightness of his hopes; and which twelve years had left unchanged, except to mature the loveliness of earliest youth into more womanly beauty and expression, and to deepen the pensiveness, that always marked it, into a shade of habitual melancholy.

"Adèle, are *you* too leagued against me?" resumed La Tour, with recovered firmness, and looking stedfastly on her; "have *you* entered into the secret counsels of my foe? and are you sent hither to torture me with your presence? to remind me, by it, of past, but never to be forgotten, injuries — of the worse than infernal malice, with which he has ever pursued me, and for which, I exult in the hope of one day calling him to a deadly reckoning!"

"Speak you thus of my husband?" she asked, in an accent of reproof; "and think you such language is meet to be addressed to the ear of a wife?"

"Aye, of your husband, lady," said La Tour, yielding to his chafed and bitter feelings; "he was once my friend, too; the friend who won my confidence, only to abuse it, who basely calumniated me, in absence, who treacherously stole from me the dearest treasure of my heart. Adèle," he continued more calmly, "I do not love you *now*; that youthful passion, which was once the sun of my existence, has lost its strength in other ties, and sterner duties; but, can I meet your eye again, and not recall the perfidy which drove me forth, from friends and country, an adventurer in the pathless wilderness? can I look upon your face, and not curse the wretch, who won from me its smiles, who burst our love asunder, in all its purity and fervor, while yet unruffled by one shade of doubt, one fear of disappointment?"

"La Tour," said Mad. d'Aulney, striving to conceal her emotion, "why all this bitter invective? now, indeed, most vain and useless! why wound my ear, by accusations which *I* surely do not merit, and which is a most ungrateful theme, when uttered against one whom I am bound, by every tie of duty and interest, to respect! If you believe me innocent" —

"I do believe you are most innocent!" interrupted La Tour, impetuously; "yours was a heart too guileless to deceive, too firm in virtuous principle to be sullied, even by a union with the vicious and depraved. No, Adèle, I have never cherished one feeling of resentment towards you; you, like myself, was the victim of that baseness, which invented a tale of falsehood to deceive you, of that meanness, which flattered your father's ambitious hopes, by a boast of rank and wealth; while my only offer was a sincere heart, my only wealth, an untarnished name, and a sword, which I hoped would one day gather me renown, in the field of honor."

"Enough of this," said the lady, exerting all her firmness; "it is unwise to recall the past, nor is this a fitting time to indulge in reminiscences of pain or pleasure; the night is fleeting fast, and every moment of delay is attended with danger."

"What mean you?" asked La Tour, a sudden hope of release darting through his mind; "*I* fear no danger; but *you* may well dread a tyrant's wrath, should you be seen hovering around a prison, which he would be loath to cheer with one ray of brightness."

"I must first see you depart," she replied; "and then, I trust, the good saints will guide me safely back to the couch of my sick infant, from which I stole, when every eye was closed in sleep, to attempt your liberation."

"My liberation!" said La Tour, in surprise; "may heaven bless you for the kind thought, Adèle; but you deceive yourself, if you admit the possibility of effecting it."

"You know not my resources," she answered, with a smile; "but listen to my plan, and you will no longer remain incredulous; I am persuaded the chance of success is much greater than the danger of discovery, and unless we *do* succeed, I fear you will have much, and long to suffer."

"There is no chance which I would not hazard," said La Tour, "to free myself from this hateful prison, which is more intolerable to me than the most hopeless dungeon ever invented by despotic jealousy. Yet I would endure any sufferings, rather than involve *you* in difficulty, or for an instant expose you to the suspicion of one, too unrelenting, I well know, to extend forgiveness, even to those who have the strongest claims on his tenderness."

"Passion and prejudice render you unjust," said Mad. d'Aulney; "but this hour and place are too dangerous to authorize idle scruples, and what is to be done can admit of no delay. Yet I will first remove your apprehensions on my account, by assuring you, that my husband thinks me ignorant of your situation, and, of course, my interference in your escape cannot be suspected." She blushed deeply as she added, "from whatever cause, he has carefully concealed your imprisonment from me, and induced me to believe, that a lieutenant, only, led on your people to the engagement with him, and that he was the present occupant of this apartment. I need not add, that the transient glimpse I accidentally obtained of you, undeceived me, and that I have confined this discovery entirely to my own breast."

"Dastard!" exclaimed La Tour, indignantly; "this jealous care accords well with the baseness of his heart; and I wonder not that he fears to lose the affection which was so unjustly gained, if, indeed, it were ever truly his."

"Must I again ask you, La Tour," she said, with a displeased air, "to refrain from these invectives, which I may not, cannot listen to, and which render my attempt to serve you, almost criminal?"

"Forgive me this once only, madam," said La Tour, "and I will endeavor not to offend again. And now, will you have the goodness to impart your plan to me; and, if you are excluded from blame and danger, how shall I bless the generous courage which prompted you to appear in my behalf!"

"My confessor has been ill for several days," said Mad. d'Aulney; "and, during his confinement, two missionary priests, attached to the settlement, have frequently attended him, and been permitted to pass the gates without questioning, whenever they chose. Early this morning, I encountered a priest, of very peculiar appearance, whose person was entirely unknown to me; he was going to the sick man's apartment, and, I have since learned, supplied the place of one who usually attended, but had unexpectedly been called away. There was something in his tall figure, and the expression of his pale and melancholy features, which arrested my attention; I closely remarked him, and perceived that he looked round inquisitively, though he wore an air of calm abstraction, which would scarcely have been suspected by an indifferent observer."

"It must have been father Gilbert," said La Tour; "and, if he is concerned, I would place the utmost confidence in his prudence and fidelity."

"That is his name," said Mad. d'Aulney, "as I was afterwards told by Antoine, the guard, who now waits at the door" —

"Antoine! *he* cannot be trusted," interrupted La Tour; "he has once deserted my cause, and joined the standard of an enemy, and I cannot again rely on his integrity."

"He was seduced from his duty," returned Mad. d'Aulney; "but, I believe, has sincerely repented of his error, and is now anxious to atone for it. You shall judge for yourself. A few weeks since, he was so dangerously ill, that very faint hopes were entertained of his recovery; and, hearing that he was a stranger, and in many respects destitute, I was induced to visit him, and administer such comforts as his state required. What he termed my kindness, excited his warmest gratitude, and he unburthened his conscience to me, of the crime which seemed to lie heavily on it. He considered his disorder a visitation of Providence, inflicted as a punishment for his desertion; and he wished most earnestly to return to your service. I was pleased with the good feelings he displayed, but advised him to rest contented for the present, promising to aid his wishes if any opportunity offered; and, from that time I have seen little of him, till since your arrival."

"And you have now engaged his assistance?" asked La Tour; "well, be it so; once more in the open air, I fear not even treachery; and, furnished with a trusty weapon, I bid defiance to every obstacle that can oppose my freedom."

"Caution you will find more useful than strength," said Mad. d'Aulney; "and by its aid we have thus far succeeded, even beyond my expectations. This afternoon, I observed father Gilbert in conversation with Antoine; and, trusting to the sincerity of the latter, I soon after found a pretext for speaking with him, and cautiously introduced the subject of your escape. He was ready, at every risk, to assist in any measures which could be adopted; and informed me that it had already been discussed between himself and the priest, and that he was, this night, to stand sentinel at your door. Nothing could be more propitious to our views; and, in the course of the day, we have found means to arrange every thing, I hope, with perfect safety."

"This is indeed a kindness, a condescending interest, of which I am wholly unworthy," said La Tour, with energy; "how,

Adèle, can I ever show you the gratitude, the" —

"Speak not of that, La Tour," she hastily interrupted; "think now of nothing but your safety; trust implicitly to the guidance of Antoine; and, I trust, it will soon be insured."

"And you," said La Tour, "who have generously hazarded so much to aid me — how can I be satisfied that you will escape unharmed? how can I leave you, in uncertainty and peril?"

"Believe me," said Mad. d'Aulney, "I am perfectly secure; Antoine will desert his post to go with you, and suspicion must rest entirely on him, and father Gilbert. The priest waits for you without the fort; and, once with him, pursuit will be unavailing, even if your flight is soon discovered; delay no longer, the morning watch approaches, and you must be far from hence, before another guard appears to relieve Antoine. These garments will sufficiently disguise you," she added, divesting herself of a loose robe and monkish cloak, which covered her own dress; "the soldier on duty will take you for a priest returning from the confessor's room, and you will probably pass unquestioned, as the priests, of late, have free access here at all hours."

"And whither do you go, and how elude observation?" asked La Tour.

"I have only to cross the passage, and descend a narrow staircase," she replied; "both of which were left to the vigilance of Antoine; and I shall reach my own apartment, without encountering any one."

A low rap was at that moment heard without the door; Mad. d'Aulney, at the sound, turned quickly to La Tour, and offering him her hand, with a melancholy smile, she said,

"It is time for us to part; and may the blessed saints be with you, St. Etienne, and guide you from hence in safety; we may never meet again, but my prayers will always intercede for your happiness and prosperity."

"God bless you, Adèle," said La Tour, in a subdued voice, taking her hand respectfully, "for this night's kindness; for all that you have ever shewn me, words are too feeble to express my gratitude; may heaven watch over you, and make you as happy as you deserve to be: farewell!"

Mad. d'Aulney turned from him in silence; and Antoine instantly opening the door, in obedience to a signal from her, she addressed a parting word of good will to him, and hastily descended the stairs. La Tour stood with his eyes fixed on her retiring figure, till Antoine ventured to urge his departure, by reminding him, that every moment's delay increased the danger of discovery. He started at the suggestion; and, wrapping the cloak around him, and drawing the cowl closely over his face, they proceeded in perfect silence, leaving the door secured, as before, by bolts and bars, in the hope that it might lull suspicion for a short time, or, at least, retard the moment of certain discovery. They passed out into the open air, through a door which Antoine had the means of opening, and thus avoided the sentinels who guarded the usual passage.

The continued darkness favored La Tour's disguise; they safely reached the gate, and Antoine informed the guard that he was ordered to conduct the holy father out, and that he had, himself, a commission from his lord, which would detain him several hours. They were immediately permitted to pass. Every obstacle was then surmounted, and, with feelings of exultation, La Tour again stood upon the ocean's verge, and listened to the rushing of the wind and waves, beneath the free and ample canopy of heaven. He looked back towards the fort, visible by a few glimmering lights, and the gratitude and tenderness which had so recently subdued his stern and haughty spirit, were strangely blended with revenge and hatred against the man, from whose power he was then escaping.

Antoine uttered a shrill whistle, which was answered by the dash of oars; and a skiff presently shot from a little bay, and drew near the spot where they waited. Father Gilbert was in it; La Tour grasped his hand, in silence; and Antoine, taking the oars, applied all his strength and dexterity, to bear them swiftly over the dark and troubled waters.

CHAPTER XV.

Who is't can read a woman?
SHAKSPEARE.

Arthur Stanhope found M. de Valette at Pemaquid, according to the information of father Gilbert; for the priest had, in fact, left him there on the preceding evening, and it was from him that he learned the tidings of La Tour's imprisonment.

Soon after his interview with Stanhope, at Mount Desert, father Gilbert obtained permission to visit the confessor at Penobscot, during the absence of a priest who usually attended him; nor did this voluntary act of charity excite any suspicion against one who had gained so high a reputation for zeal and sanctity. Antoine saw, and instantly recognized him; and, suspecting that his visit to the fort was prompted by a wish to learn the situation of La Tour, he, under the seal of confession, imparted his yet immature plan of escape, and, almost beyond his hopes, found in him a very able assistant and adviser.

Father Gilbert was aware that La Tour favored the Hugonot cause; but he, with reason, doubted the sincerity of his motives; for he encouraged the Catholic religion throughout his settlement, and supported the authority of the priests. He knew that Mad. de la Tour was warmly attached to the protestant cause, and that her influence was extensive; the establishment of the true-faith, therefore, seemed to depend on La Tour's support and assistance; and if some measures were not soon adopted to procure his freedom, D'Aulney would probably detain him long in confinement, or perhaps send him to France, to await the slow process of a trial. If any feelings of personal regard towards La Tour influenced the priest, they were unacknowledged even to his own heart; for he carefully excluded every earthly object from his affections, and seemed to endure life, only in the hope that a severe and constant discharge of his sacred duties would, at length, insure him a happy release from its painful bondage.

Towards the close of the day preceding La Tour's escape, De Valette received a message from father Gilbert, requiring him to return, without delay, to the neighbourhood of fort Penobscot. Though he assigned no reason for his request, nor gave any intimation of his plans, the young Frenchman reposed implicit confidence in his discretion; and, moreover, as a good Catholic, he was so habituated to the control of a spiritual guide, that he did not hesitate a moment to comply with this desire. Stanhope was rather surprised at this ready submission on the part of De Valette, which was, by no means, a prominent trait in his character; but, as nothing could be gained by remaining at Pemaquid, he consented to accompany him, on his nocturnal voyage.

The wind favored their passage, but the evening was dark and gloomy; and, with no certain object in view, their progress was tedious in the extreme. The vessels kept close in company, but it was after midnight when they reached the place appointed by father Gilbert; and, presuming that they should hear nothing from him till morning, they anchored near each other, off the shore of Mount Desert. The morning twilight was just breaking on the distant hills, when the watch from De Valette's vessel descried an approaching boat. It was occupied by three persons, two of them labored at the oars, and the third sat in the midst, with folded arms, in a state of perfect immobility.

"That is father Gilbert, but who brings him hither?" exclaimed De Valette, as they drew up to the ship's side, and pulled in their oars. La Tour sprang upon the deck, flinging aside the disguise which he had till then retained; and a shout of joyful recognition was echoed by every voice in either vessel. Antoine was received on board with enthusiasm; and, in answer to the eager inquiries which poured from every lip, La Tour briefly related the circumstances of his escape, though he carefully suppressed any allusion to the assistance of Mad. d'Aulney. It was long before the tumult of gratulation subsided; but father Gilbert, who alone remained cold and unconcerned, retired from it as soon as possible, and resumed the guidance of his little bark, which had safely borne him on many a solitary voyage. The chant of his matin hymn rose, at intervals, on the fitful breeze; and Stanhope watched him till he disappeared behind the point of land round which he had followed him on the preceding day.

La Tour, convinced that all the force which he could at present command was insufficient to contend with D'Aulney, whose strength had been greatly, though perhaps without design, misrepresented to him, ordered the sails to be set for a homeward voyage; and, before sunrise, the shores of Penobscot were left far behind them.

The remainder of the night, which succeeded La Tour's release, was passed by Madame d'Aulney, in a state of morbid excitement. She watched alone by the side of her sleeping infant, and even maternal solicitude was, for a time, suspended by the intense interest, which her own perilous adventure, and the safety of La Tour awakened. She felt that she had done a deed, for which, if by any chance discovered, she could never hope to obtain forgiveness from her incensed husband. Still, her conscience acquitted her of any motive criminal in its nature, or traitorous to his real interest; and the reflection that it had been in her power to confer an essential benefit on the man whom she had once deeply, though most unintentionally, injured, was inexpressibly soothing to her feelings. She counted the moments, which seemed to linger in their flight, and started at the slightest sound, till sufficient time had elapsed to convince her that he must have proceeded far on his way, towards a place of safety.

The dreaded discovery was indeed deferred beyond her utmost expectations. The guard, who was to relieve Antoine, repaired to his post at the appointed time; and, though surprised to find it vacated, yet as the door was perfectly secure, he contented himself with uttering an oath at his comrade's negligence, and in a few moments it was almost forgotten. An hour or more passed away, and no motion was heard within; morning advanced — he thought it strange that his prisoner should enjoy such sound repose, and a suspicion of the truth began to dawn upon his mind. He unbarred the door, and his suspicions were, of course, instantly realized. Repenting the easy faith which had suffered him to delay an examination, he hastened to impart the intelligence, which soon spread dismay and confusion throughout the garrison.

Madame d'Aulney heard the loud voices, and hurried steps of the soldiers without, and the quick note of alarum, whose fearful summons could not be mistaken. These sounds, though long expected, struck heavily on her heart; and she uttered a fervent petition to the Virgin, to speed the wanderer on his doubtful way. She heard various reports of what had taken place, from her attendants; but she prudently waited for the storm of passion to subside, before she ventured into the presence of M. d'Aulney, conscious that the utmost effort of self-command would be necessary to meet his eye with her usual composure.

"Methinks you are tardy this morning, madame!" he said, stopping in his hurried walk, and looking fixedly on her countenance, as she at length entered the room where he was alone.

"Our sick child must plead my excuse," she replied; "he still requires a watchful care, and I am unwilling to consign him to any one less interested than myself."

"You are a fond mother," said D'Aulney, resuming his walk; "but, there are few husbands who choose to be neglected for a puling infant."

"The duties of a wife and mother are closely blended," she returned; "and I trust I have not been deficient in the performance of either."

"You well know," he said, peevishly, "that I have no fancy for the nursery, with its appendages of children and nurses; and yet, for three days, you have scarcely condescended to quit it for an instant. Yes, for three days," he repeated, again stopping and looking earnestly at her, "you have secluded yourself from me, and your cheek has grown pale, as if some cherished care, or deep anxiety, had preyed upon your thoughts!"

"And what anxiety can exceed a mother's?" she asked, the tears springing to her eyes; "what care so ceaseless and unwearied, as her's, who watches over the helpless being to whom she has given existence; whose sufferings no other eye can comprehend; whose infant wants demand the constant soothings of her enduring tenderness, and exhaustless love! And has this excited your displeasure?"

"My own affairs have chafed me, Adèle," he said, more gently; "a favorite project has miscarried, and the vengeance I have so long desired is foiled, in the very moment when I believed success undoubted; all this, too, through my own easy credulity, and a lenity, which its object ill deserved from me!"

"You have erred on the safer side," said Madame d'Aulney, timidly; "and your own heart, I doubt not, will acknowledge, in some cooler moment, that it is far better to forego the momentary pleasure of revenge, than to commit one deed which could stain your name with the guilt of tyranny and oppression."

"You know little of the wrongs," he answered, sternly, "which for years have goaded me; and which, if unrevenged, would brand me with worse than a coward's infamy. The artifice, which has so often baffled my plans; the arrogance, which has usurped my claims; even you, gentle as you are, would scorn me, if I could forgive them!"

"Mutual injuries require mutual forgiveness," she replied; "and, in the strife of angry passions, it is not easy to discriminate the criminal from the accuser. But," she added, seeing his brow darken, "you have led me into a subject which can only betray my ignorance; you well know that I am wholly incompetent to judge of your public affairs; and I have never ventured to obtrude upon your private views, or personal feelings."

"You have too much of a woman's heart, Adèle," he said, "to become the sharer of important councils; a freak of fancy, or a kindly feeling, might betray or destroy the wisest plan that could be formed."

"Nay," she answered, smiling, "I have no wish to play the counsellor; and it is well, if my husband can be satisfied with the humble duties which it is my sole ambition to fulfil."

"And there are enough of these within the limits of our own household," D'Aulney replied; "though you are but too ready to extend your benevolent exertions beyond; you were, for instance, most zealous, the saints only know why, to save the life of that scoundrel soldier of La Tour's, when he lay sick here; — I would that he had died! — and, trusting to your commendations, and his apparent honesty, I raised him to my favor, and gave him a post, which he has but now most basely betrayed. Fool, that I was, to think he could have served with such a master, and not bring with him the taint of treachery!"

"Poor Antoine!" said Madame d'Aulney, equivocally; "he made fair professions, and the most suspicious could not have doubted his sincerity. *You* did not *then* object to my rendering him those slight services, which, you thought, might attach him more strongly to your cause; and I could not think he would repay me with ingratitude. But I marvel that you, who are so habitually wary and discerning, should have been deceived by his pretensions; the friend, or servant, who has once proved perfidious, is unworthy any future confidence."

D'Aulney started, as if stung by the last remark, and looking keenly on her, replied,

"He is not the only traitor whom I have fostered and protected; some other hand has been busy in this work, and, though it were the dearest that I have on earth, my wrath should not abate one tittle of its justice."

"It was, indeed, a bold adventure!" said Mad. d'Aulney, with admirable composure; "but if, as I am told, a priest gained access to the prisoner through Antoine's intervention, they would scarcely deem it necessary to run the hazard of employing any other agency; and let us not be guilty of injustice, by indulging suspicions of the innocent."

"I have closely questioned the father confessor on this subject," he replied, thoughtfully; "and I learn that a stranger, one of his own crafty order, yesterday visited him; and that soon after leaving his apartment, he was observed in close conference with the wretch Antoine; but the guard denies admitting any one through the gate at a later hour; though a priest, or, as is now supposed, the prisoner in his garb, passed out after midnight, with the deserter, who gave some plausible excuse for departing at that unseasonable hour."

"The men are terrified by your anger," said Mad. d'Aulney, "and probably contradict each other in their natural eagerness to justify themselves; you permitted the priests to enter freely, and no one can be blamed for obeying your commands, which did not prohibit a stranger under the sacred habit."

"The confessor's illness," resumed D'Aulney, with bitterness, "has gathered all the priests in the land around him; and this goat, who entered with the herd, is doubtless a creature of La Tour's; but, beshrew me, were the holy father in the last extremity, I would not admit another, without a scrutiny which no artifice could escape."

"You have many prisoners left," said Madame d'Aulney, carelessly; "and this one, though the chief, was he so very important as to justify all this severity?"

"It matters not, madame," he answered, sternly; "but I care not to have my wishes thwarted by cunning; my plans defeated by fraud and artifice. Yet your curiosity shall be gratified," he added; "or, tell me, do you not already know who has so narrowly escaped the punishment his crimes have well deserved?"

"You told me," she replied, "that it was a lieutenant of M. de la Tour's, and I have, of course, sought no further information."

"It is well that you did not;" he said, hastily; "but suppose I should now tell you that it was the miscreant, La Tour himself, would that palliate the severity of which you are so ready to accuse me?"

"It would not extenuate the subterfuge which at first concealed the truth from me," she answered, with an indignant blush, "nor atone for a want of confidence, which I had not deserved from you."

"And of what importance was this mighty secret to *you*?" he asked, sarcastically; "methinks you should rather thank me for the kindness which saved you" —

"It was well," she interrupted, in an accent of decision, "and now let it pass forever. Your kind precaution, fortunately, has prevented some suspicions, which, I perceive, you were but too ready to indulge."

"I yet trust he has not quite escaped;" resumed D'Aulney, after a moment's pause; "I have sent out parties in every direction through the neighbouring country, and swift boats across the bay; and he must be gifted with almost supernatural powers, to elude pursuit. His return shall be loudly celebrated," he added, with a gloomy smile; "and you shall not complain, Adèle, that we do not call you in to the rejoicings!"

"I think he will avoid giving that triumph," she replied; "for he doubtless anticipated your pursuit, and was prepared to elude it; some of his own people were, most probably, in concert with the priest, to secure him a safe retreat."

"I doubt not that you wish it," said D'Aulney, angrily; "that you rejoice in his success, though it abolish my fairest schemes, and prolong a conflict which has already proved pernicious to my fortune and interests."

"I can wish for no event," she answered, mildly, "which would retard your honorable designs, and defeat any rational prospect of happiness or advantage; neither can I adopt prejudices which I do not comprehend, or wish evil to one who has never injured me."

"It is well, madame," he replied; "and your benevolence, perchance, will be rewarded. But, though he now escape, believe me, the hour of vengeance will one day arrive; I will follow him till he surrenders the possessions so unlawfully retained, and ceases to assume a power which has no longer an existence, but in name."

"And is it for a name only, that you contend?" asked Mad. d'Aulney; "must our domestic peace and safety remain in jeopardy, and the din of strife forever ring around us, because a powerless enemy refuses to yield imaginary rights?"

"You are wilfully ignorant on this subject," he replied; "and shew little of that submission, which a dutiful wife should feel for her husband's judgment; but it is enough that I know the justice of my own cause, and that I bear a sword, which has ever been faithful to its trust. Go you," he added, tauntingly, "and count your rosary, and mutter to the saints a prayer with every bead; it may be they will protect the traitor, whom your good wishes have already followed."

So saying, he abruptly left the room; and Madame d'Aulney, with tearful eyes, and an oppressed heart, hastened to the retirement of her own apartment.

CHAPTER XVI.

I cannot love him;
Yet I suppose him virtuous, know him noble.

*   *   *   *   *

—— —— *but yet I cannot love him,*
He might have took his answer long ago.

SHAKSPEARE.

Rumors of M. de la Tour's defeat and capture, attended with the usual exaggerations, were not slow in reaching fort St. John's; and they could not fail of producing a strong excitement in the garrison, and of rendering those more closely connected with him, deeply anxious respecting the result. Madame de la Tour had been attacked by a severe illness, from which she was slowly recovering; and Luciè dreaded to impart to her the tidings, which from her own feelings, she was assured would excite the most painful solicitude. But her aunt's penetrating eye soon detected the concealment, and she could no longer withhold a minute detail of the reports which had reached her ears. They were, however, received by Mad. la Tour with unexpected firmness. She could not, indeed, suppress her uneasiness, but she felt that exertion was necessary, and, from that moment, the languor of disease yielded to the energy of her mental courage.

Madame de la Tour had experienced many vicissitudes, and, as the wife of a soldier of fortune, she had learned to bear success with moderation, and to meet reverses with fortitude. She loved her husband, and with a spirit as high and undaunted as his own, and a mind far more noble and generous, she cherished his honor, as the only treasure which violence or injustice could never wrest from him. Affection is always credulous, and fortunately for her happiness she gave no belief to the high charges which were publicly alleged against him; but placed the most undoubting trust in his assurance, that they were the baseless calumnies of an enemy. Even the many dark shades in his character, which could not escape her discernment, she was ever ready to palliate; and her bland influence often restrained the violence of his stern and vindictive temper.

La Tour, with all his faults, was never unjust to her merits; and, though he had married her without affection, her exemplary conduct gradually removed his indifference, and gained an ascendancy over him, which his pride would never have brooked from a less superior mind. The misfortune which had now befallen him, Mad. de la Tour had reason to apprehend, would lead to still more serious consequences. His imprisonment might prove long and perilous; and it was probable that D'Aulney would take advantage of so good an opportunity to renew his attempt upon the fort. La Tour had drawn his best men from the garrison, in the sanguine hope that he was leading them to victory; and now that defeat and capture had befallen them, those who remained behind were dispirited by the apprehension of an attack, for which they were entirely unprepared. Madame de la Tour again appeared amongst them; and, though pale and debilitated by recent illness, her presence inspired them with renewed hope and resolution. Her directions were obeyed with an alacrity, which shewed their confidence and affection; and she had soon the satisfaction of finding every duty promptly fulfilled, and every precaution taken, which the most vigilant prudence could suggest. These arrangements, and their attendant cares, necessarily engrossed much of her time and thoughts; and diverted her mind from the contemplation of her husband's dreary situation.

Several days passed away, and no intelligence was received, which could tend to relieve her anxiety. A few of the men who escaped from the wreck of Stanhope's vessel had returned to St. John's, and confirmed the report of that disaster; but they were ignorant of any events which afterwards took place, either with regard to him, or La Tour. Lucièendeavoured to support the irksome suspense, with something of that equanimity which her aunt invariably exhibited. But she was less practised in this species of self-control; and the silence, which Madame de la Tour preserved respecting Stanhope, increased her uneasiness and depression. She had never alluded to him, except in some casual remark, since the evening of his departure; and Lucièhad no reason to believe her sentiments respecting his attachment were at all changed. Pride and delicacy restrained her from entering on a theme, which was so pointedly shunned; but she felt wounded by a reserve that she had never before experienced; and the silence imposed on her, only gave more activity to her thoughts, which were perpetually engrossed by a subject, so closely connected with her happiness. Mad. de la Tour's conduct towards her was in every other respect unchanged; her affection and confidence undiminished; and Luciè fancied she could discern, in this, the influence of her guardian's prejudices, or, perhaps, a prohibition which her aunt would not venture to disregard.

Two or three days of gloomy weather had confined Madame

de la Tour almost entirely to her own apartment; tidings long expected were still delayed; and, in spite of every effort, the disappointment and anxiety evidently depressed her spirits. On the first return of sunshine, she proposed a walk with Luciè, to the cottage of Jacques and Annette, which stood at a little distance without the fort, and had been presented to them, on their marriage, by La Tour, as a reward of their fidelity. It was at the close of a balmy day, in the early part of autumn; and, for a time, they walked on in silence, each one engrossed by her own reflections. Madame de la Tour at length abruptly said,

"This soft and fragrant air brings healing on its wings! my strength and spirits are already renovated by its soothing influence, and even inanimate nature seems rejoicing in this brilliant sunshine, so doubly welcome, after the damp and heavy fogs, which have so long hung round us!"

"It is almost like the mild, transparent evenings of our own bright clime," said Luciè; "but *there* we can enjoy, without the fear of perpetual change, while in this land of vapors, the sun which sets with most resplendency often rises shrouded in clouds."

"It is this contrast, which gives a piquancy to all our pleasures," said Mad. de la Tour; "no sky is so serene, as that which succeeds a tempest; and a slight alloy of sorrow or disappointment gives a zest to subsequent enjoyment."

"No one can love variety better than I," said Luciè, smiling; "provided its shades are all reflected from glowing colors; but I would prefer a calm and settled enjoyment, however monotonous it may seem, to those sudden bursts which borrow half their brightness from the contrasted gloom of a reverse!"

"You will find nothing permanent in this changeful world, Luciè; and, from your exuberant gaiety, wisely reserve a portion of cheerfulness, at least, to support you, in the darker moments of misfortune, which the most favored cannot always escape. I have had my share of them; and it is not a trifling evil, that my husband is now a prisoner, in the hands of his most deadly enemy; but it is weakness to indulge in useless regrets and apprehensions, and I have only to perform my duty faithfully, and cherish the hope, that his own courage, or the assistance of his friends, will soon effect his rescue."

"We have but too much reason to believe, that they are all sharers of his captivity," returned Luciè; "had De Valette, or any of them escaped, they would surely have returned hither, before this time."

"They would scarcely be welcome here," said Mad. de la Tour, "if they returned, before they had done all that brave men could do, to recover the liberty of him, whom they have pledged themselves to serve!"

"Their own feelings, I doubt not," replied Luciè, "would prompt them to use every exertion to effect that object, and Eustace's courage, we know, is unquestioned. We have heard, too," she added, with slight hesitation, "that Mr. Stanhope procured another vessel, after his disaster, to go on and assist my uncle; and if, as is possible, he and De Valette are still at liberty, it would be strange indeed, if their united efforts proved unavailing."

"I have no reason to doubt the courage or sincerity of Mr. Stanhope," said Mad. de la Tour; "but it is most natural to place our chief reliance on those whom we have long known and regarded; and Eustace is certainly more deeply concerned in the honor and safety of his uncle, than a stranger possibly can be."

"His personal feelings may be more strongly interested," replied Luciè; "but where honor or duty is involved, I believe Stanhope would peril his life against that of the bravest man in Christendom."

"Your good opinion of this English stranger," her aunt coolly replied, "seems rather to increase; but absence is a deceitful medium, particularly when the object viewed through it is invested with the attractions of a foolish partiality."

"Absence has never influenced my feelings on this subject," said Luciè, deeply coloring; "my opinion of Mr. Stanhope has been the same, from the earliest period of our acquaintance."

"It is strange," said Madame de la Tour, "that, for so long a time, you should have refrained from mentioning even the name of this valued friend to me; that you should have permitted the affection of De Valette to gain encouragement and strength, when you were resolved to disappoint it; and that too, from a romantic attachment, which you had little hope of realizing, and blushed to acknowledge!"

"I have no reason," replied Luciè, "to blush for an attachment which was honorably sought, and bestowed on a worthy object; but involved, as it long was, in uncertainty, maidenly pride forbade the confession, even to *you*; and De Valette surely had no reason to expect it from me! Without this motive, my regard for him never could have exceeded that of a friend, or sister; my conscience acquits me of having shewn him any ungenerous encouragement; and, if he suffers disappointment, he must seek the cause in his own pertinacious vanity, which led him to believe his pretensions irresistible."

"It may rather be found in your own caprice, Luciè; a caprice which would lead few young women to reject an alliance in every respect so advantageous."

"Had I no other objection to De Valette," said Luciè, "I should be most unwilling to connect myself so closely with one, whose religious principles are directly at variance with those which I have been taught from childhood to reverence; my dear aunt Rossville often spoke to me on this subject, and almost in her last moments, warned me never to form an alliance which might endanger my faith, or expose me to the misery of finding it scorned by him to whom I had entrusted my happiness, and whose views and feelings would never unite with mine, on a subject of the highest concern and importance."

"That objection might be rational in most instances," said Madame de la Tour; "and no prospect of temporal advantage for you, I am sure, would induce me to urge a step which could expose you to such trials, or jeopardize those principles, which you well know I have always inculcated, and most highly prized. But De Valette is no bigot, and I am persuaded he would never counteract your inclinations, or restrain you from worshipping according to the dictates of your conscience. Both your parents, as you already know, Luciè, were Catholics; many of your father's connexions are now high in favor with the ruling party, and your marriage with a Catholic would doubtless be agreeable to them; and, while it established your own fortune, might give you an opportunity to serve the cause of our persecuted sect."

"I feel under no obligations to my father's relations," replied Luciè; "they have never shewn any interest in me; even my existence has seemed a matter of indifference to them, and there is scarcely one to whom I have been personally known."

"There were some peculiar circumstances connected with your father's history," said Mad. de la Tour, "which, for a long time, involved his nearest friends in deep affliction. He did not long survive your mother, and his family would gladly have received you into their protection, had not your aunt Rossville claimed you as her sister's last bequest. She soon after became a protestant, and persisted in educating you in that faith, which naturally gave offence to your paternal relatives; and to that cause alone I attribute the decline of their interest. But, if you return to France, and as the wife of De Valette," —

"That I can never do!" interrupted Luciè; — "dearest aunt," she added, "I would sacrifice much to gratify your wishes; but the happiness of my whole life, — surely you would not exact that from me!"

"I exact nothing from you, Luciè," she replied; "but I would have you consider well, before you finally reject the tried affection of De Valette, and with it affluence and an honorable station in your native land, merely from the impulse of a girlish fancy, which would rashly lead you from friends and country, to share the doubtful fortunes of a puritan; to adopt the habits of strangers, and endure the privations of a youthful colony!"

"I have reflected on all these things," said Luciè; "and I am persuaded that wealth and distinction are, at best, but empty substitutes for happiness; and that the humblest lot is rich in true enjoyment, when shared with one whose love is the fountain of our hopes, whose smile can brighten the darkest hour, and scatter roses over the thorniest path of life. I had rather," she added, with a glowing cheek, "far rather trust my little bark to the guidance of affection, upon the placid stream of domestic joy, than to launch it on the troubled waters of ambition, with pleasure at the helm, and freighted with hopes and desires, which can bring back no returns but those of disappointment and vexation."

"This is a dream of idle romance, which can never bear the test of reality," said Mad. de la Tour; "and I hope you will detect its fallacy before you are taught it by the bitter lessons of experience."

"Our opinions on this subject," said Luciè, "I fear must remain entirely at variance; but, as I have yet many months left for reflection, let us at present suspend the discussion. Here is Annette's cottage; and, if you please, I will extend my walk a little, and return when I think you are sufficiently rested from your fatigue."

Madame de la Tour readily assented to her proposal; and Luciè, guided by that delightful association of thought and feeling, which leads us to retrace, with so much pleasure, the scenes where we have lingered with those we love, directed her steps to a wooded bank, which overhung the water, where she had last parted from Arthur Stanhope. The sun was setting with unwonted splendor, and the bright reflection of his golden beams tinged the cloudless sky with a thousand rich and varied hues, from the deep purple which blended with his crimson rays, to the pale amber, and cerulean tint, that melted into almost fleecy whiteness. The earth glowed beneath its splendid canopy, and the trees, which skirted the border of the bay, threw their lengthened shadows upon the quiet waves, which lay unruffled and bathed in the glory of the gorgeous heavens.

Lucièstood on the very spot where she had received the last adieu of Stanhope, and the same objects which now met her eyes, were the mute witnesses of that parting scene. Every leaf that trembled around her revived some cherished remembrance; and the breeze, which sighed through the foliage, was soft as the voice of whispered love. But painful conjectures respecting his present situation, at length engrossed every thought; and the recollections of happiness, and dreams of hope, were alike absorbed in the suspense and anxiety which, for many days, had gathered gloomily around her. She involuntarily glanced across the bay, as if expecting that some messenger would approach with tidings; and she started with joyful surprise, on observing a vessel just below, and, at that moment, on the point of anchoring. She gazed earnestly for a short time, and her heart throbbed audibly as she saw a small boat leave its side and steer directly towards the fort; two persons were in it, and the dark flowing garments of father Gilbert could not be mistaken.

Love, it is said, though notoriously blind in the main, is quick-sighted on such occasions; and another glance assured Luciè, that the companion of the holy father, who plied the oars with so much diligence, was no other than Arthur Stanhope. The little boat glided swiftly on its course; it soon neared the shore, and Luciè screened herself behind a clump of trees, when she found it verging to a cove, hard by, which formed a sheltered harbour for such light vessels.

CHAPTER XVII.

I cannot be
Mine own, nor any thing to any, if
I be not thine; to this I am most constant,
Though destiny say, no.

SHAKSPEARE.

Arthur Stanhope soon guided his boat into the cove, and leaped on shore, followed more leisurely by father Gilbert, who proceeded alone to the fort. Stanhope lingered behind, apparently enjoying a profound reverie, while, step by step, he approached the grove where Luciè was still concealed. Her habitual dread of father Gilbert induced her to remain silent, till he was out of sight; when she bounded lightly from her covert, and stood before her lover. An exclamation of delighted surprise burst from his lips, as he sprang eagerly towards her; and it was several moments before the joyful excitation of mutual and happy emotions admitted of calm inquiry and explanation.

"You must now tell me, Arthur," Luciè at length said, "what miracle has brought you here; how you have escaped from storms, and shipwreck, and captivity, and all the evils which we heard, I fear too truly, had befallen you!"

"Report, I perceive, has at least multiplied my misfortunes," he answered, smiling; "I have been in no danger from the sword or prison, and, though the tempest treated my poor vessel roughly, thanks to its mercy! we all escaped with life, and, therefore, have no reason to complain."

"That dreadful night and day!" said Luciè, with a shudder; "did I not tell you, Stanhope, that a storm was gathering? and when we stood together on this very spot, and I pointed to the heavy clouds, and sullen waves, you only smiled at my fears, and paid no heed to my predictions!"

"I knew not, then, that you were so skilled in reading the mystery of the clouds," he answered; "and if I had, dear Luciè, I fear that knowledge would have availed me little; my honor was pledged in the undertaking, and I could not delay it, even to gratify the wishes, which you urged with so sweet a grace, and an interest so flattering."

"Well, let it pass," she replied; "you are safe again, and we need not the tempest's aid to enhance the sunshine of this moment. And now tell me, where you have left my uncle, and De Valette, and all who went out with you, in such a gallant show? and why you have returned alone, or only with that dreaded priest, who seems to traverse earth and sea, like a spirit, gifted with ubiquity?"

"But this dreaded priest, Luciè, whom you regard with so much fear, appears inclined to use his mysterious influence for benevolent purposes; and Mons. de la Tour is certainly much indebted to his exertions for being so soon freed from imprisonment."

"My uncle *is* free and safe, then?" asked Luciè, "though, indeed, your looks before assured me of it; and I ought not to have delayed so long imparting the intelligence to my aunt. Suffer me to go, Stanhope; you know not her anxiety!"

"You will not leave me so soon, my dearest girl?" he asked, again drawing her arm through his; "indeed, it is useless; father Gilbert has by this time reached the fort, and imparted all that you could, and much more, with which you are yet unacquainted."

"But my aunt is not there, Stanhope; I left her at Annette's cottage; and, I doubt not, she already thinks it strange that I have not returned: if she knew that I was loitering here with you" —

"She would not think it *very* strange," interrupted Stanhope, smiling, and still detaining her; "and, in the happy tidings of her husband's safety, even you, Luciè, may be for a time forgotten. If the priest is mortal, as I must believe he is, though you seem to doubt it, he will probably feel some pleasure in communicating good news, and I owe him this slight satisfaction, for the favor he conferred in bringing me hither."

"I do not yet understand," said Luciè, "why you are here alone, or where you have left the companions of your luckless expedition? I hope you have not entered into a league with the priest, or acquired any of his supernatural powers?"

"No, Luciè," he replied; "I shall long remain contented with the humbler attributes of mortality, rather than acquire any powers which can make you flee from me. The mystery is very easily solved, as I doubt not, all which pertains to the holy father might be. Released from all our difficulties, I left Penobscot Bay, in company with La Tour; we were vexed with head winds, for a day or two, against which my vessel, being small, was enabled to make greater progress, and leaving him behind, I just now anchored yonder, waiting for the tide to proceed up to the fort. But I was too impatient to see you, to remain at that short distance another moment; and as father Gilbert chanced to make his appearance just then, I availed myself of his boat to convey me here; for he chose to land at this place instead of going on to the fort. I could not pass this spot without pausing an instant, to recall the moment when I last saw you. I knew this was your favorite hour for walking; and, smile if you will, something whispered me, that I might again meet you here."

"My solitary rambles are not always directed to this spot," she answered, with a conscious blush; "and it was mere chance that brought me here this evening. But, perhaps," she archly added, "absence has seemed so brief to you, that you expected to find me lingering where you left me!"

"Absence from *you* seem brief!" he said; "I would that you could read my heart, Luciè; you would there find how dark is every hope, how cheerless every scene, how lengthened every moment, which is not shared with you! Deem me not presumptuous," he added, "when I ask, why we should part again? why delay the fulfilment of those hopes, which you have permitted me to cherish, and doom me to the misery of another separation!"

"Do not urge me on this subject, Arthur," she replied; "the reasons which I once gave you, still exist; nor can any arguments diminish their force, nor any motives induce me to reject their influence. Nay, your brow is clouded now," she added, smiling; "as if you thought caprice or coldness moved me to refuse your wishes; and yet your heart must tell you, I am right, and that it is not kind in you to seek to draw me from my duty."

"Convince me, first, that it *is* your duty, Luciè, and I will not urge you more; I will then yield, cheerfully, if I can, to those scruples which, I confess, now appear to me fastidious."

"You are wilfully perverse, Arthur, but it will require more time than I can at present command, to convert you to my opinion; you see, even this bright twilight is fading from us, and my aunt will be uneasy at my long absence; indeed you must not detain me another moment."

"You will at least suffer me to go with you Luciè," —

"I cannot," she interrupted; "Annette's cottage is near, and I fear nothing; besides, here is my shaggy page," she said, pointing to the large dog which followed her; "and he is as trusty in his office, as any that ever attended the steps of a roving damsel."

"And he enjoys the privilege of shewing his attachment," said Stanhope, coloring; "while I am restrained, even from those slight attentions which common civility demand! I am weary of this secrecy, Luciè, and nothing but your urgent wish could have compelled me to endure it so long!"

"My prohibition is now withdrawn," she replied; "not because you have borne it with so much patience, but because my aunt detected the secret, and drew from me a confession, which, in truth, I should have made voluntarily, had I not feared it might involve her in my guardian's displeasure."

"And that smile, dear Luciè, assures me, that the avowal was not ill-received."

"My smile is deceptive then," she answered; "no, Arthur, unjust as it may appear to you, as it most certainly does to me, my aunt is vexed and disappointed at what she chooses to consider my perverse inclinations; and though I am persuaded she would never interpose her authority to prevent my wishes, her consent to them will not be very readily obtained. You were, but just now, the subject of our conversation, and I left her displeased with the opinions I had ventured to express; I fear your unexpected appearance with me so immediately after, might not be well received, and this is my sole objection to your returning with me."

"I have certainly no wish to obtrude myself in any place," said Stanhope; "and particularly where my presence could excite displeasure against you: and, though I feel convinced that the sentiments imbibed against me are most unjust, yet if your favor, your affection may I add, dear Luciè, survive their influence, I will not repine at that injustice which gives an added proof to its strength and constancy."

"I thought it was already proved beyond a doubt!" she answered; "surely that regard which time, and almost hopeless absence, could only render more devoted and enduring cannot be endangered by the assaults of idle prejudice or the lures of mercenary ambition! My heart is more credulous in its faith than your's, Arthur; and no jealous fear could ever lead me to distrust the truth and fervor of that love which you have pledged to me!"

"And, think you, dearest girl, that I repose less confidence in you? that I can doubt the heart in which is treasured every hope and fond affection of my soul? From you, pure and disinterested as you are, I have nought to fear; but I cannot look upon the dreary blank of absence, and not feel all the misery, the thousand nameless ills, which that one word comprises!"

"Speak not of it, Arthur; it is not wise to fancy evils which may never have existence, or which, if they are in store for us, Providence has wisely hidden from our view. You see that I am strong in courage, and too chary of my present happiness, to suffer one gloomy cloud to shade its fleeting brightness!"

"Fleeting, indeed!" he answered, "another day, or two, at most, and if you still decree it, we part for many long and tedious months!"

"So soon!" said Luciè, her cheek changing with emotion; "so very soon, Arthur? why this unexpected haste, this quick departure?"

"You cannot ask me to remain here, Luciè, when to all but you, my presence is a burthen; when every other eye meets me with a coldness and distrust, which, even for your sake, I cannot longer endure! La Tour but ill concealed his feelings while he thought my services might be useful to him; but now, I can no longer aid his cause, and I will not tax him even for the poor civility he has so grudgingly bestowed!"

"You are right," said Luciè; "and under such circumstances I cannot even wish you to prolong your stay; but when we next meet, Arthur" —

"When we next meet, Luciè? would that we were not to part! that I could now prevail on you to unite your fate with mine, and shun the contingencies of another dreaded separation!"

"It is in vain to ask it, Arthur," she replied; "it would only hasten the opposition and strife of angry feelings, which I would not provoke, till I feel at liberty to obey the dictates of my own will. My guardian has now a right to prevent my choice, and I have no doubt he would exercise it to the utmost; but when I am freed by law from his authority, he will cease to importune me on a subject so entirely unavailing. My promise also is pledged to my aunt, that I will not even enter into an engagement without her sanction, before that period."

"And what is her object in requiring this promise?" asked Stanhope; "is it not in the hope that she shall prevail with you, in my absence, to become the wife of De Valette?"

"Perhaps it is," said Luciè; "but do not suffer this idea to give you one moment's uneasiness; — no, Arthur, believe me, neither threats nor entreaties can change the purpose of my mind, or diminish that affection, which will ever remain as fervent and unchanged, as if the most sacred promise was given to pledge my fidelity, or the most holy vows already united our destinies."

At that moment they reached a green pathway, leading to Annette's cottage; and Luciè again reminding Stanhope that he must leave her, he felt compelled, reluctantly, to turn into another direction, and pursue his lonely way to the fort.

Madame de la Tour, in the mean time, had scarcely heeded Luciè's protracted absence, as she sat at the cottage door, enjoying the fragrance and beauty of the evening, which her late confinement rendered peculiarly grateful. The last glow of twilight faded slowly away, and the falling dews began to remind her, that she had already lingered beyond the bounds of prudence. She was surprised that Luciè stayed so inconsiderately, and at length became seriously uneasy at her delay. But her anxiety was for a time diverted, by the appearance of Jacques, who came in haste from the fort, with the intelligence which father Gilbert had just communicated, that La Tour was at liberty, and then on his homeward voyage.

Mad. de la Tour immediately left the cottage, persuaded that Luciè must have returned without her. She had not proceeded far, when she encountered father Gilbert, walking with his usual slow and measured steps, and a countenance perfectly abstracted from every surrounding object. She had never spoken with the priest, for her peculiar tenets led her to regard his order with aversion; nor had she before particularly noticed him. She now saw in him only the messenger of her husband's freedom; and, eager to make more particular inquiries, she hastily approached him, though with a degree of reverence which it was impossible for any one to avoid feeling in his presence. The priest stopped, on finding his progress thus impeded, and looked coldly on her; but gradually his expression changed, the blood rushed to his face, and a sudden brightness flashed from his piercing eyes. The lady, engrossed by her own feelings, did not observe the change, but, in a tone of anxious inquiry, said,

"Holy father, you are a messenger of good tidings, and I would crave the favor of hearing them confirmed, from your own lips!"

With startling energy, the priest seized her hands, and fixing his eyes wildly on her, exclaimed,

"Lady, who are you? speak, I conjure you, while I have reason left to comprehend!"

"I am the wife of Mons. de la Tour," she answered, terrified by his strange conduct, and vainly striving to free herself from his grasp.

"The wife of Mons. de la Tour!" he repeated; "no, no, you are not; — you would deceive me," he added, vehemently; "but you cannot; those features ever, ever haunt me!"

"For whom do you mistake me?" asked Madame de la Tour, with recovered self-possession, but still deadly pale.

"Mistake you!" he answered, with a shudder; "no, I know you well — I thought you would return to me! you are" — he lowered his voice, almost to a whisper, and spoke with calm emphasis, "you are Luciè Villiers!"

"My God!" exclaimed Mad. de la Tour, "who are you? No,"

she quickly added, "I am not Luciè Villiers, but I am the sister of that most injured and unhappy lady."

"Her sister!" said the priest, striking his hand upon his forehead, with a perplexed air; "I thought it was she herself; — yet, no, that could not be. Her sister!" he repeated, wildly; "and do you not know me? not know the wretched, miserable De Courcy?"

A piercing cry from Madame de la Tour followed these words, and attracted the attention of Jacques, who was standing before his cottage door. He flew to assist his lady, but, before he reached her, she had sunk, senseless, on the ground, and father Gilbert was standing over her, with clasped hands, and a countenance fixed and vacant, as if deserted by reason. Jacques scarcely heeded him, in his concern for Mad. de la Tour; he raised her gently in his arms, and hastened back to the cottage, to place her under the care of Annette; when he returned, soon after, to look for the priest, he had disappeared, and no traces of him were found in the fort or neighborhood.

CHAPTER XVIII.

"How hast thou charm'd
The wildness of the waves and rocks to this?
That thus relenting they have giv'n thee back
To earth, to light and life."

Luciè, immediately after parting with Stanhope, chanced to meet father Gilbert, as he was hurrying from the spot where he had just held his singular interview with Madame de la Tour. She avoided him, with that instinctive dread of which she could never divest herself on seeing him; and he passed on, without appearing to notice her, but with a rapidity too unusual to escape her observation. She found Annette's quiet cottage in the utmost confusion, occasioned by the sudden illness of Madame de la Tour, who had then scarcely recovered from her alarming insensibility. Luciè hung over her with the most anxious tenderness, and her heart bitterly accused her of selfishness, or, at best, of inconsideration, in having been induced to prolong her absence. But her aunt did not allude to it, even after her consciousness was entirely restored; she spoke lightly of her indisposition, attributing it entirely to fatigue, though her sad and abstracted countenance shewed that her mind was engrossed by some painful subject. She made no mention of father Gilbert; and Luciè, of course, did not feel at liberty to allude to him, though Annette had told her of their conference, and her curiosity and interest were naturally excited to learn the particulars. It could not but surprise her, that Mad. de la Tour should have been in earnest conversation with the priest; for she had always shunned him, and ever treated Luciè's fears as some strange deception of the imagination.

M. de la Tour returned late in the evening of that day; but the shock which his lady had received, whether mental or physical, again confined her several days to her apartment. Luciè was convinced that this renewed indisposition was, in some manner, connected with the appearance of father Gilbert. She, at length, ventured to speak of him to her aunt; but the subject evidently distressed her, though she confessed his peculiar manners had at first alarmed her; adding, with an attempt at gaiety, that he was probably scandalized at being so abruptly addressed by a female and a heretic. With apparent indifference, she also asked several questions of Luciè, respecting her accidental interviews with the priest; thus betraying a new and uncommon interest, which strengthened the suspicions of her niece. These suspicions were soon after confirmed, by casually learning that La Tour had himself made strict inquiries concerning father Gilbert; but he had withdrawn himself, no person knew whither; though it was supposed to some of the solitary haunts he was in the habit of frequenting.

Day after day passed away, the subject was not renewed, and other thoughts gradually resumed their ascendancy in Luciè's mind. Stanhope had returned to Boston, and previous to his departure he sought an interview with La Tour, and formally requested the hand of Luciè. His suit was, of course, rejected, though with unexpected courtesy; her guardian alleged, that he had other views for her, which he considered more advantageous; but expressed the highest personal regard for him, and the utmost gratitude for the services he had so freely rendered. When La Tour, however, found that Luciè was really fixed in her attachment to Stanhope, and resolved against a marriage with De Valette, he could not suppress his angry disappointment; and his manner towards her became habitually cold, and often severe. Luciè deeply felt this ungenerous change, but without noticing it in the slightest degree; and, indeed, it was partly compensated by the kind attentions, and even increased affection, of her aunt, who, though not perfectly reconciled to her choice, no longer sought to oppose it.

Madame de la Tour recovered but slowly from her unfortunate relapse; and De Valette, endeavoring to hide his mortification and chagrin, under an assumed reserve, was no longer the gay and constant companion of Luciè's amusements and pursuits. She was thus left much alone; but, fortunately for her, she possessed abundant springs of happiness in the resources of her own mind, and the unclouded gaiety of her spirits; and every lonely hour, and each solitary spot, glowed with the bright creations of hope, or responded to the thrilling chords of memory. All her favorite walks had been shared with Stanhope; there was scarcely a tree which had not sheltered them; and every gushing stream, and forest dell, even the simplest flower which spread its petals to the sun, breathed in mute eloquence some tale of innocent enjoyment. These scenes, which his presence had consecrated, where, in the freshness of dewy morn, at noontide's sultry hour, and beneath the still and moonlight heavens, she had admired, with him, the loveliness of nature, were now retraced, with the enthusiasm of a fond and devoted heart.

Such feelings and reminiscences had, one day, drawn her into the green recesses of a forest, which stretched along the river, at some distance above the fort. The familiar and oft-frequented path, wound through its deepest shades, beneath a canopy of lofty pines, whose thickly woven branches created a perpetual twilight. She at length struck into a diverging track, and crossing a sunny slope, bared by the laborious settler for future improvement, reached a steep bank, which declined gently to the water's edge. It was one of those cheering days in early autumn, which sometimes burst upon us with the warmth and brilliancy of summer, and seem, for a brief space, to reanimate the torpid energies of nature. The sun glowed in mid-day fervor, and myriads of the insect tribes, revived by his delusive smile, wheeled their giddy circles in the light, and sent their busy hum upon the calm, clear air. The wild bee, provident for future wants, had sallied from his wintry hive, and sipped from every honied cup, to fill the treasures of his waxen cell; and a thousand birds of passage folded their downy pinions, and delayed their distant flight, till bleaker skies should chill their melody, and warn them to depart.

Luciè threw herself on a grassy knoll, beneath a group of trees, completely sheltered by the broad leaves of a native grape-vine which climbed the tallest trunk, and leaping from tree to tree, hung its beautiful garlands so thick around them, as to form a nat-ural arbor, almost impervious to the brightest sun-beam. The opposite shore of the river was thickly wooded, chiefly with those gigantic pines for which that province is still famed; but inter-spersed with other trees, whose less enduring foliage was marked by the approach of early frosts, which had already seared their verdure, and left those rich and varied tints that charm the eye in an autumnal landscape, while yet too brilliant to seem the presage of decay. The river flowed on its still smooth course, receiving on its waves the reflection of nature, in her quiet but ever glorious array, and mingling its faint murmurs with the busy sounds which breathed from those countless living things, that sported their brief existence on its banks.

Not far above the spot where Luciè reclined in the luxury of dreaming indolence, the river was contracted by a ledge of rocks, through which the stream had worn a rough and narrow channel. The full waters of the noble river, arrested by this confined and shallow passage, rushed violently over the steep and craggy rocks, and pouring their chafed and foaming current into the calm stream, which again expanded to its usual width, produced a fall of singular and romantic beauty. Every rising tide forced back the waters from their natural course, precipitating them into the stream above with equal rapidity, though from a less appalling height. Twice, in each tide, also, the sea was on a level with the river, which then flowed smoothly over the rocks, and at those times only, the dangerous obstruction was removed, and the navigation unimpeded.

Luciè had remarked the waters as unusually placid, on first approaching the bank, and she did not advert to this perpetual change, till their loud and increasing murmurs had long fallen unheeded on her ears. Her attention was at length aroused; and though she had often witnessed it before, she gazed long, with unwearied pleasure, upon the troubled stream, as it bounded from rock to rock, dashing with impetuous fury, and tossing high in air its flakes of snowy foam. The report of a fowling piece, at no great distance, at length startled her; and a well-known whistle, which instantly succeeded, assured her that the sportsman was De Valette. She had wandered from the shade of the grape vine to obtain a more distinct view of the falls; but not caring to be seen by him, she hastily plunged among a thicket of trees, which grew close to the water's edge. The place was low and damp; and in looking round for a better situation, her eye fell on a bark canoe, which was drawn in among some reeds; and, without hesitation, she sprang into it, and quietly seated herself. It was probably left there by some Indian, who had gone into the woods to hunt, or gather roots; a neat blanket lay in it, such as the French often bartered for the rich furs of the country, and several strings of a bright scarlet berry, with which the squaws were fond of decorating their persons.

Luciè, in the idleness of the moment, threw the blanket around her, and twined some of the berries amongst her own jet black hair. She had scarcely finished this employment, when she heard quick approaching footsteps, and, glancing round, saw De Valette pushing heedlessly through brier and bush, and Hero trotting gravely at his side. A loud bark from the dog next foreboded a discovery; but both he and his master had halted on the summit of the bank, apparently to survey the occupant of the boat. Luciè's curiosity was aroused to know if he would pass on without recognizing her; and busying herself in plaiting some reeds, which she plucked from beside her, she broke into a low chant, successfully disguising her voice, and cautious that no words should be distinguished, except one or two of the Indian dialect, which she had learned from an old squaw who frequented the fort.

"How now, my little squaw," said De Valette, advancing a few steps; "have you got cast away among the reeds?"

"I am waiting for the tide, to take me down to the fort," she answered, in such unintelligible French, that he could scarcely comprehend her.

"And what are you so busy about?" he enquired, approaching near, to satisfy his curiosity.

"Making a basket; and I will give it to you for some beads, when it is done!" said Luciè, in the same imperfect jargon, stooping her head low, and concealing her hands lest their delicacy should betray her.

But Hero, who had listened, and observed with his usual acuteness, interrupted the farce at that moment by springing to the boat, and placing his fore paws in it, he gently seized the blanket in his mouth, and pulled it from her unresisting shoulders. A bark of pleasure succeeded this exploit, as he laid his shaggy head in her lap, to receive the expected caress.

"Now, by my faith, mademoiselle," said De Valette, coloring with mingled feelings, "I can indeed, no longer discredit your pretensions to the art of disguise."

"Indeed, you have no reason to do so," she said, smiling; "though I scarcely thought, Eustace, that you had less penetration than your dog! But do you remember what I once told you; — twice deceived, beware of the third time!"

"I would not have believed *then*, Luciè, that you were so skilled in deceit!" he said, in a tone of bitterness; but quickly added, carelessly, "I willingly confess that I have not penetration enough to detect the disguises of a woman's heart!"

"It would certainly be difficult to detect that which has no existence," said Luciè, gaily; "we are but too guileless, too single-hearted, in truth, for our own happiness."

"And for the happiness of others, you may add," rejoined De Valette; "the boasted simplicity of your sex is so closely allied to art, that, by my troth, the most practised could scarce detect the difference!"

"I begin to have faith in miracles," said Luciè, with arch gravity; "surely nothing less than one could transform the gallant De Valette, the very pink of chivalrous courtesy, into a reviler of that sex, who" —

"Who are not quite so faultless as my credulity once led me to believe them," interrupted De Valette.

"Nay, if you have lost your faith in our infallibility," she answered, "your case is hopeless, and I would counsel you to put on the cowl, at once, and hie away to some dull monastery, where you can rail, at leisure, against woman and her deceptive attributes. It might form a new and fitting exercise for the holy brotherhood, and, methinks, would sound less harshly from their lips, than from those of a young and generous cavalier."

"I am not yet so weary of the world as to avail myself of your advice," he replied; "however grateful I may, feel for the kindness which prompts you to give it."

"I hope you do feel more gratitude than your looks express," said Luciè; "for, though I have labored most abundantly to please you, I cannot obtain one smile for my reward."

"You have never found it difficult to give me pleasure, Luciè," returned De Valette; "though unhappily I have been less fortunate in regard to you."

"You are petulant today, Eustace," she said; "or you would not accuse me so wrongfully; nay, you have been very, I must say it, very disagreeable of late, and followed your own selfish amusements, leaving me to wander about alone like a forsaken wood-nymph. Indeed, it is neither kind nor gallant in you."

"And can you think I have consulted my own inclinations, in doing so?" he asked, with vivacity. "Believe me, Luciè, my heart is ever with you, and when I have been absent or neglectful, it was only from the fear of obtruding those attentions, which I thought were no longer prized by you."

"You have done me great injustice, by admitting such a thought, Eustace," she replied; "and I appeal to your own conscience, if any caprice or coldness on my part, has given you reason to imagine that my feelings toward you have changed."

De Valette colored highly, and paused a moment, before he replied;

"I have no inclination to complain, Luciè, but you have long known my sentiments too well to suppose I could view with indifference your acknowledged preference for another, and it was natural to believe that preference would diminish the interest which I once had the presumption to hope you entertained for me."

"No circumstances can ever diminish that interest, Eustace," she replied; "our long tried friendship, I trust, cannot be lightly severed, nor the pleasant intercourse which has enlivened the solitude of this wilderness be soon effaced from our remembrance: believe me," she added, with emotion, "whatever fate awaits my future life, my heart will always turn to you, with the grateful affection of a sister."

"A sister!" De Valette repeated, with a sigh; and the transient flush faded from his cheek, while he stooped to caress the dog, which lay sleeping at his feet.

A moment of embarrassing silence ensued, which Luciè broke, by asking De Valette if he was returning to the fort, and proposing to accompany him.

"If the owner of this canoe was here to row us," she continued, "I should like extremely to return in it, the water looks so cool and inviting, and I am already weary."

"It would be madness to venture against the tide, in that frail vessel," replied De Valette; "and, indeed, Luciè, I think your present situation is not perfectly safe."

The tide was, in fact, rising with that rapidity so peculiar to the Bay of Fundy, and which, of course, extends, in some degree, to the rivers that empty into it; and while Luciè occupied the canoe, it had, unnoticed by her, been nearly freed from the reeds, which, a short time before, had so effectually secured it. She observed that a wider space of water separated her from the land; and, striking one end of a paddle upon the sandy bottom, to support her as she rose in the rocking bark, she reached the other hand to De Valette, who stood ready to assist her in springing to the shore. A slight dizziness came over her, caused by the constant but scarce perceptible motion of the canoe, and alarmed on feeling it dip to the water's edge as she was on the point of leaping, she pressed forcibly against the oar, while the corresponding motion of her feet impelled the boat from the shore, with a velocity which instantly precipitated her into the waves.

This scene passed with such rapidity, that De Valette fancied her hand already within his grasp, when the giddy whirl and heavy plunge struck upon his senses, and the flutter of her garments caught his eye, as the waves parted and closed over her. Eustace was an indifferent swimmer; but, in the agony of his terror, every thing was forgotten but Luciè's danger; without hesitation he threw himself into the stream, and exerted all his skill to reach her, when she soon again appeared, floating on with a swiftness which seemed every instant to increase the distance between them. He heard the din of waters rushing over the rocks, and knew that he was hastening towards the fearful gulf, from the loud and still increasing noise which they sent forth, as they dashed across the narrow channel. The thought that Luciè's fate was inevitable, and most appalling, if he could not save her before she reached that fatal spot, redoubled his exertions, which, however, every effort only rendered more faint and ineffectual.

Happily for Luciè, extreme terror had deprived her of consciousness, and she was borne unresistingly on the rapid waves, ignorant of the peril which surrounded her. She already seemed within the vortex of the cataract; and its confused and deafening clamor for an instant recalled her senses, and thrilled coldly through her heart. But she was suddenly drawn back by a powerful grasp, and when she again opened her eyes, she was lying on a grassy bank; the melody of the woods chimed sweetly around her, and the distant tumult of the waves fell, softened to gentle murmurs, on her ear. A confused recollection of danger and escape crossed her mind; but the feelings it excited were too overwhelming, in her exhausted state, and she again sunk into complete insensibility.

Luciè owed her recovered life to the generous exertions of an Indian, who, returning to his canoe, the unlucky cause of her misfortune, was attracted by her perilous situation. He swam to her rescue with a dexterity acquired by long and constant practice, and reaching her at a moment when death seemed inevitable, succeeded in bearing her safely to the shore. With scarcely a moment's respite, he returned to the assistance of De Valette, who was completely subdued by his efforts, and must have sunk, but for the aid of his faithful dog. The animal, with equal courage and attachment, persevered in holding him securely, and was, in fact, dragging him towards the shore, when the Indian came to his rescue, and conveyed him to a place of safety. His first anxious inquiries were respecting Luciè; and his gratitude to his deliverer was enhanced by the knowledge, that he had been the preserver of her life also. The disinterested exertions of the poor Indian were most warmly acknowledged, and liberally rewarded, both by De Valette and Luciè.

When Luciè recovered from her long insensibility, she found herself supported in the arms of some one, who seemed watching over her with the utmost solicitude. She at first gazed vacantly on his face; but, as her recollections became more vivid, she started and uttered a faint cry, recognizing the features of father Gilbert. The expression of his countenance was gentle, even to softness, and his eyes were evidently moistened with tears. He, however, released her, on finding her consciousness fully restored, and removing to a little distance, remained standing in perfect silence. Luciè in vain attempted to speak: the priest, as he continued to look on her, became deeply agitated; he again approached her, and pronounced her name in a voice of tenderness, though trembling with emotion. Luciè's habitual dread of him was lost in the powerful interest which his altered manner and appearance excited; her imploring eyes demanded an explanation, and he seemed about to speak, when the loud bark of Hero was heard, and he bounded towards her, followed by De Valette and the Indian.

Father Gilbert hastily retired, and was soon hid in the deep shadows of the forest.

CHAPTER XIX.

"Oh Jealousy! thou bane of pleasing friendship,
Thou worst invader of our tender bosoms;
How does thy rancor poison all our softness,
And turn our gentle natures into bitterness."

A few hours of repose restored Luciè's exhausted strength; though the appalling danger from which she had been so providentially rescued, left a far more enduring impression on her mind. The evening of that day was serene and cloudless, and the breeze which floated from the river had nothing of the chilliness so usual at that season. Luciè sat at an open window, her eyes fixed on the curling waves, which glanced brightly beneath the moon, whose silver beams were blended with the lingering rays of twilight. An expression of deep and quiet thought marked her countenance, though the mental suffering she had so recently endured might still be traced in her pale cheek, which was half shaded by the ringlets of jetty hair, that fell profusely around it. Her forehead was reclined on one hand, the other rested on the head of Hero, who sat erect beside her, as if conscious that his late intrepid conduct entitled him to peculiar privileges.

Madame de la Tour was seated at a little distance, removed from the current of evening air which her delicate health would not permit her to inhale, and evidently suffering that extreme lassitude, which usually follows any strong excitement. Both remained silent: each apparently engrossed by thoughts which she cared not to communicate to the other. The silence was at length abruptly broken, by an exclamation from Luciè, of "Father Gilbert!" uttered in an accent so quick and startling, that Mad. de la Tour sprang involuntarily from her musing posture, and even the dog leaped on his feet, and looked inquiringly in her face.

"Poor Hero! I did not mean to disturb you," said Luciè, patting her dumb favorite, and rather embarrassed, that she had unwarily produced so much excitement.

"Father Gilbert!" repeated Mad. de la Tour; "and is he coming hither again?"

"No, I saw him but an instant," said Luciè; "and he has now disappeared behind the wall."

She hesitated, and still kept her eyes fixed on her aunt's face, as if wishing to ask some question, which she yet feared might not be well received.

"What would you say, Luciè?" asked Mad. de la Tour, with a

faint smile; "I perceive there is something on your mind, which you would fain unburthen; and why should you hesitate to speak it to me?"

"Perhaps it is an idle curiosity, dear aunt," she replied; "but you asked if father Gilbert was coming hither *again*, as though he had already been here; and, I confess, I am anxious to learn if I understood you correctly?"

"You did, Luciè; and you will be more surprised when I assure you, that I held a long conference with him this morning: one too, in which *you* are particularly concerned."

"*I* concerned! *you* hold a conference with father Gilbert!" said Luciè, in unfeigned astonishment; "dearest aunt, I entreat you to explain yourself."

"The explanation must necessarily be long, Luciè," she replied; "and as I know your feelings will be deeply excited, I fear the agitating events of this day have scarcely left you strength and spirits, to bear the recital. Tomorrow" —

"Oh, now, dear aunt!" interrupted Luciè; "I am well, indeed, and can bear any thing better than suspense. I too, have seen the priest today, and his look, — his manner was so changed, yet still so unaccountable, that he has not been since one instant from my mind."

"Where did you see him, Luciè?" asked Mad. de la Tour; "and why should you conceal the interview from me?"

Luciè, who, till this incidental recurrence to father Gilbert, had avoided mentioning even his name, since she found the subject so embarrassing to her aunt, gladly relieved her mind, by relating the particulars of her rencontre with him in the morning, and described the deep interest with which he seemed to be watching her recovery. Madame de la Tour listened attentively to her recital, but apparently without surprise; and after a short pause, which was evidently employed in painful reflection, she said,

"It is time that all this mystery should be explained to you, Luciè; for, what I have so long attributed to the influence of your imagination, is now more rationally accounted for, though until a few hours since, I was, myself, ignorant of many facts, which I am about to relate to you. But I must first beg you to close the window; the air grows cool, and I should also be loath to have our discourse reach the ears of any loiterer."

Luciè obeyed in silence; and drawing her chair closer to her aunt, she prepared to listen, with almost breathless attention.

"I must revert to the period of your mother's marriage,

Luciè," said Madame de la Tour, "and, as briefly as possible, detail those unhappy circumstances which so soon deprived you of her protecting love. You will no longer be surprised that I have repressed your natural curiosity on this subject; for it must excite many painful feelings, which I would still spare you, had not a recent discovery rendered the disclosure unavoidable."

"The subject agitates you, my dear aunt," said Luciè, observing her changing complexion with anxiety; "you are indeed too ill, this evening, to make so great an exertion, and I had far rather wait till another day, when you will probably be better able to bear it."

"No, I am well now," she replied; "and will not keep you any longer in suspense." She then resumed,

"Your mother, Luciè, had the innocence and purity of an angel; she was gay, beautiful, and accomplished, — the idol of her friends, the admiration of all who saw her. That picture, which you so often gaze on with delight, is but a faint resemblance of what she was. The lineaments are indeed true to nature, but no artist could catch the ever varying expression, or imbody that unrivalled grace, which threw a charm around her, more captivating even than her faultless beauty. She was just four years older than myself, but this difference of age did not prevent the closest union of sentiment and feeling between us; and, as she was almost my only companion, I early renounced my childish amusements for the more mature employments, which engaged her attention. We lived much in retirement; my father was attached to literary pursuits, and devoted himself to our education; a task which he shared with my eldest sister, who was many years our senior, and affectionately supplied the place of our mother, who died a few months after my birth.

"Your mother, Luciè, was scarcely sixteen when she first saw Mons. de Courcy. Chance introduced him to our acquaintance, as he was travelling through the province where we then resided; her loveliness attracted his admiration, and he soon avowed a deeper and more impassioned sentiment. Till then she had never dreamed of love; it was reserved for him to awaken its first emotions in a heart susceptible of the most generous and devoted constancy, the most fervent and confiding tenderness, exalted by a delicacy and refinement, which could only emanate from a mind as virtuous and noble as her own.

"De Courcy had already passed the season of early youth, and his disposition and feelings were, in many respects, extremely opposite to your mother's. His figure was commanding, his features regular and expressive; though, on the whole, he was remarked rather for the uncommon grace and elegance of his deportment, than for any of the peculiar attributes of manly beauty. His manners were cold, and even haughty, in his general intercourse with society; but, with those whom he loved and wished to please, he was gentle and insinuating; and when he chose to open the resources of his highly gifted mind, his conversational talents were more versatile and fascinating, than those of any individual whom I have ever known. There was a cast of deep thought, almost of melancholy, in his countenance, which was ascribed, I know not if correctly, to an early disappointment; but it was seldom banished, even from his smiles, and often increased when all around him seemed most gay and happy. His feelings, indeed, were never expended in light and trifling emotions; they were strong, silent, and indelible; and those who viewed the calmness of his exterior, little dreamed of the impetuous passions which slumbered beneath, and which he was accustomed to restrain by the most rigid and habitual self-command. Some of these traits excited my father's solicitude for the future happiness of his daughter; but they were overbalanced by so many noble qualities and shining virtues, that no other eye detected their blemishes. Your mother believed him faultless; she had given him her affections, with all the enthusiasm of her guileless heart; and he regarded her with a devotion, that almost bordered on idolatry."

Madame de la Tour paused, and Luciè, raising her head from the attitude of profound attention with which she listened, asked, in an accent which seemed to deprecate an affirmative answer,

"You are not weary, I hope, dearest aunt?"

"Not weary, Luciè," she replied; "but you must sometimes allow me a moment's respite, to collect and arrange my thoughts. More than twenty years have passed since these events, yet, child as I then was, they made too deep an impression on my mind to be effaced by time; and I cannot, even now, reflect on them without emotion.

"I have dwelt thus minutely on your father's character," she continued, "that you may be prepared for" —

"For what?" interrupted Luciè; "surely all these happy prospects were not soon darkened by clouds!"

"We will not anticipate," said Mad. de la Tour, in a voice slightly tremulous. She again resumed,

"De Courcy was the younger son of an ancient and honorable family. My sister's rank and fortune equalled his expectations, her beauty gratified the pride of his connexions, and the endearing qualities of her mind and heart won their entire approbation and regard. Their marriage was solemnized; and never was there a day of greater happiness, or one which opened more brilliant prospects for futurity. De Courcy conveyed his bride immediately to a favorite estate, which he possessed in Provence, whither I was permitted to accompany them; and six months glided away, in the full enjoyment of that felicity which their romantic hopes had anticipated. Winter approached, and your father was importuned to visit the metropolis, and introduce his young and beautiful wife to the gay and elevated station which she was expected to fill.

"Your mother, accustomed to retirement, and completely happy in the participation of its rational pleasures, with one whose taste and feelings harmonized entirely with her own, yielded, with secret reluctance, to her husband's wishes, and exchanged that peaceful retreat, for the brilliant, but heartless scenes of fashionable life. The world was new to her, and no wonder if her unpractised eye was dazzled by the splendor of its pageantry. She entered a magic circle, and was borne round the ceaseless course with a rapidity which threw a deceitful lustre on every object, and concealed the falseness of its colors. She became the idol of a courtly throng; poets sung her praises, and admirers sighed around her. Her heart remained uncorrupted by flattery; but, young and inexperienced, buoyant with health and spirits, no wonder that she yielded to the fascinations which surrounded her, or that her thoughts reverted less frequently, and less fondly, to those calm pleasures which had once constituted her only happiness. Her affection for her husband was undiminished; but the world now claimed that time and attention, which, in retirement, had been devoted to him; and, engrossed by amusements, every intellectual pursuit was abandoned; and domestic privacy, with its attendant sympathies and united interests, was, at length, entirely banished.

"De Courcy, chagrined by a change, which his experience in life should have enabled him to foresee, became melancholy and abstracted; he often secluded himself from society, entrusting his wife to some other protection, or, when induced to enter scenes which had become irksome to him, he watched, with jealousy, even the most trifling attentions that were offered her. He, who possessed such a heart, should never have doubted its truth, or wounded her affection by distrusting its fervor and sincerity. He had led her into the fatal vortex, and one word from him could have dissolved the spell; the slightest expression of his wishes, would, at any moment, have drawn her from pleasures of which she already wearied; and, amid the sweet tranquillity of nature, they might have regained that happiness, which had withered in the ungenial atmosphere of artificial life. But he was too proud to acknowledge the weakness he indulged; and when she besought him, even with tears, to explain the cause of his altered conduct, he answered her evasively, or repulsed her with a coldness, which she felt more keenly than the bitterest reproaches. Confidence, the strongest link of affection, was broken, and the golden chain trembled with the shock.

"Nothing is more galling to an ingenuous mind, than a consciousness, that the actions and feelings are misconstrued by those to whom the heart has been opened with that perfect trust and unreserve, which ought to place them beyond the shadow of suspicion. Your mother deeply felt the injustice of those doubts; and perhaps, a little natural resentment mingled with and augmented the pain, which rankled in her inmost soul. But, satisfied of her innate rectitude, and of that true and constant love, which even unkindness could not weaken, she left her innocence to vindicate itself, and made no farther attempt to penetrate the reserve which her husband had assumed, and which opposed a fatal barrier to returning harmony. Experience in the world, or a thorough knowledge of your father's peculiar disposition, might have suggested a different, and, perhaps, a more successful course. But she judged and acted from the impulse of a sensitive and ardent mind, which had freely bestowed the whole treasure of its warm and generous affections, and could ill brook a return of such unmerited coldness and distrust. Her conduct towards him was marked by the most unvarying sweetness, and a studious deference to his wishes; they, however, seldom met, but in a crowd; for she sought society with an eagerness, which seemed the result of choice, while it was, in reality, a vain attempt to relieve the restlessness and melancholy that oppressed her. In public, her spirits were supported by an artificial excitement, and her gaiety seemed unimpaired; but, when alone with me, the constant companion of her solitary hours, and the sole confidant of her thoughts, she yielded to the most alarming depression. Her health evidently suffered from this disordered state of mind; but she uttered no complaint, and from her husband, particularly, concealed every symptom of illness, and appeared with her accustomed cheerfulness. Strange as it may seem, her gaiety chagrined him; he fancied her trifling with, or indifferent to, his happiness, and satisfied with the pleasures which courted her, without a wish for his participation. He little knew, — for his better feelings were warped by a morbid imagination, — how gladly she would have exchanged every other blessing for one assurance of returning confidence and affection.

"Your mother's spirits faintly revived, on the approach of spring. She was weary of dissipation: the glittering bubble, which at first charmed her eye, had burst, and betrayed its emptiness. She had a mind which panted for the noblest attainments, a heart formed for the enjoyment of every pure and rational pursuit. Her thoughts continually reverted to the first happy months of her union with De Courcy; and she impatiently anticipated the moment, when they should return to those quiet scenes; fondly believing that she might there recover her husband's love, and that a new and most endearing tie would bind him more strongly to her. These soothing hopes beguiled many an heavy hour; and, but for one fatal error, one deadly passion, they might have been fully realized!"

Madame de la Tour abruptly stopped, overcome by the painful recollections which crowded on her mind; Luciè looked at her with tearful eyes, but offered no remark; and both remained silent for several minutes.

CHAPTER XX.

What deep wounds ever closed without a scar
The heart's bleed longest, and but heal to wear
That which disfigures it; and they who war
With their own hopes, and have been vanquish'd, bear
Silence, but not submission.

LORD BYRON.

Madame de la Tour at length proceeded: — "I have already told you, Luciè, that De Courcy viewed, with uneasiness, the homage which was paid your mother, though it did not exceed the usual devotion which Parisian gallantry is wont to offer at the shrine of female loveliness. He must have expected it; for no one could have been more conscious of her beauty, or more proud of possessing it. But he persuaded himself, that this adulation was too grateful to her; his affection was selfish and engrossing, and he wished her to receive pleasure from no praises or attentions but his own. She was, perhaps, as free from vanity as any woman could be, young, beautiful, and admired as herself; and if not indifferent to the admiration which her charms excited, it was but the natural and transient delight of a gay and innocent mind; her heart was ever loyal to her husband, and his society, his fond and approving smile, were far more prized by her, than the idle homage of a world.

"The young Count de — — was an object of particular dislike and unceasing suspicion to De Courcy. They were distantly related; but some slight disagreement, which had taken place at an earlier period, created a coolness between them, which was never overcome. Your mother was aware of this, and, had she more closely consulted her prudence, would, probably, have avoided the attentions of one so obnoxious to her husband's prejudices. But the Count was gay and agreeable, the versatility of his talents amused her, and he seemed to possess many amiable and brilliant qualities. His manners were courteous; his attentions never presuming; and there was a frankness in his address, which formed an agreeable contrast to the studied flattery of others around her. Yet even the most distant civilities excited your father's distrust; the Count became, every day, an object of more decided and marked aversion, and your mother could not but feel herself tacitly implicated in his displeasure. Grieved that he could doubt her affection, or the rectitude of her heart, and relying confidently on the purity of both, she resolved not to wound the Count's feelings, by yielding to an ungenerous prejudice, and her conduct and manners therefore continued unchanged.

"As spring advanced, your mother withdrew, almost entirely, from society; but the Count de — — , among a few others, was a privileged and frequent visitor at her house. One morning, De Courcy, contrary to his usual custom, had urged her to accompany him on some short excursion; and, equally surprised and gratified by the unexpected request, it was with extreme reluctance that she felt compelled, from indisposition, to decline it. Soon after his departure, however, I persuaded her to leave her apartment, for a few moments, to look at some choice exotics, which had just been brought to the house. She was still lingering to admire them, when the Count de — — was announced, through the negligence of a servant, who had been ordered not to admit any visitors. It was too late to retire, unobserved; and the usual greetings of civility were scarcely exchanged, when De Courcy abruptly entered the room. He started, on seeing his wife, who had so recently refused his request, on the plea of illness, apparently well, and taking advantage of his absence, to admit his supposed rival to an interview. Pale with emotion, he stood a moment, as if rooted to the spot; his eye, which flashed with scorn and anger, fixed alternately on each; then deliberately turned, and left the house. The Count had met his gaze unmoved, and with an expression of calm contempt; your mother, terrified by the storm of passion which his countenance betrayed, fled precipitately to her own apartment. Ill as she was, however, and trembling with apprehension, she exerted herself to appear at dinner, hoping that the true explanation would appease her husband's irritation. But he met her with a gloomy reserve, which destroyed all hope of confidence; he did not allude to what had passed; every trace of passion was gone, and she felt re-assured by a deceitful calm, that only concealed the inward struggle.

"De Courcy left the house by day-light on the following morning; no one knew whither he was gone, but we had heard him traverse his apartment through the night, and were confident he had taken no repose. A few hours of anxious suspense passed away, and your mother had just risen from her sleepless pillow, when he suddenly entered her dressing-room. I was alone with her, and never shall I forget the impression his appearance made on me. His dress was disordered, his countenance pale and haggard, and every feature marked with the deepest anguish. Your mother rose with a faint exclamation, but instantly sunk again upon her seat. He approached her, and took her hands, even with gentleness, between his own, though every limb trembled with agitation.

"Luciè," he said, with unnatural calmness, and fixing his troubled eye on her face; "I come to bid you a long, — long farewell!"

"What mean you, de Courcy?" she asked, with extreme alarm; "speak, I conjure you, and relieve this torturing suspense!"

"My honor has been avenged!" he replied, with a hoarse and rapid utterance; "and from this moment we part — forever!"

"Part! de Courcy, my husband!" she exclaimed, in a voice of agony; "tell me, what" —

"The concluding words died on her quivering lips; the sudden conflict of strong emotions could not be endured, and she sunk insensible on my bosom. Frantic with alarm, I folded my arms around her, and, unwilling to summon any witnesses, attempted to recall her senses, by administering such restoratives as were fortunately within my reach. De Courcy looked at her an instant, like one bewildered; then fiercely exclaimed,

"She loves him! see you not how she loves him?"

"Wretched man!" I said, indignantly, "you have murdered her; go, and leave us to our misery."

"My words seemed to penetrate his heart; his features relaxed, and, before I was aware of his design, he took your mother from me, and laid her gently on a couch. The tide of tenderness had rushed back upon his soul, and every soft and generous feeling transiently revived. He stood over her inanimate form, gazing on her with melancholy fondness till the tears gushed freely from his eyes, and fell on her pallid features. At that moment, as if revived by his solicitude, she half unclosed her eyelids, and a faint glow gave signs of returning life. De Courcy kissed her cold lips, and, murmuring a few words, which did not reach my ear, he gave one last and lingering look, and turned precipitately to leave the room.

"I had retreated from the couch, inexpressibly affected by a scene, which I fondly hoped was the dawn of returning happiness. He stopped, as he was passing me, and, wringing my hand with emotion, pointed to your mother, and, in a voice scarcely audible, said,

"You love her, Justine; comfort her, — cherish her, as I would have done, — God knows how fervently, — had she permitted me. Farewell, my sister, forever."

Madame de la Tour was too much agitated to proceed, and even Luciè willingly suspended the painful interest to indulge the natural emotions which her parents' history excited. After a brief interval, Madame de la Tour thus continued:

"You must suffer me to pass rapidly over the remainder of this sad tale, my dear Luciè. It was long before your mother revived to perfect consciousness; and the shock which she had received was only a prelude to still deeper misery. The conduct of de Courcy was too soon explained. Yielding to the fatal error, that she had given her affections to the Count de — —, in the excitement of his passion, he sent a challenge, which was instantly accepted. They met; and the Count was carried, as his attendants supposed, mortally wounded, from the field of contest. De Courcy, however, was spared the commission of that crime; for, though the Count's life was long despaired of, a good constitution prevailed, and he at length recovered.

"De Courcy had made all his arrangements on the preceding night; and, immediately after his interview with your mother, he quitted Paris forever. A letter was left, addressed to her, which strikingly portrayed the disordered state of his mind, and feelingly delineated the strength of his affection, and the bitterness of his disappointment. Robbed, as he believed, of her love, the world had no longer any thing to attach him; and he resolved to bury himself in some retirement, which the vain passions of life could never penetrate.

"I will pass over the agonizing scenes, the months of wretchedness which succeeded this separation, this sudden dissolution of the most sacred and endearing ties. All attempts to discover De Courcy's retreat were unavailing, though it was long before your mother could relinquish the delusive hope, that he would be again restored to her. We returned to my father's house; but there every thing reminded her of happier days, and served to increase her melancholy. Your birth was the only event which reconciled her to life; but her health was then so precarious, we dared not flatter ourselves, that she would be long continued to you. Her physicians recommended change of air, and I accompanied her to a convent on the borders of the Pyrenees, where she had passed a few years in early childhood; and she earnestly desired to spend her remaining days within its peaceful walls.

"The good nuns welcomed her to their humble retreat, in the midst of a wild and romantic solitude; and, with unwearied kindness sought to alleviate the sufferings of disease. For three months, I watched unceasingly beside her; a heavenly resignation smoothed the bed of sickness, and her wearied spirit was gently loosed from earth, and prepared for its upward flight. You were the last cord that bound her to a world which she had found so bankrupt in its promises, and this was too strong to be severed, but by the iron grasp of death. As the moment of her departure approached, she expressed a wish to receive the last offices of religion; and a messenger was sent to a neighbouring monastery of Jesuits to request the attendance of a priest. One of the brotherhood soon after entered the little cell, and the nuns, who were chanting around her bed, retired at his approach.

"I retreated unobserved, to a corner of the room, fearing she would not live through the last confession of her blameless life. A dim lamp, from which she was carefully screened, shed a sickly gleam around the apartment; and, even in the deep silence of that awful hour, the low and labored whispers of her voice scarcely reached my ear. Suddenly I was startled by a suppressed, but fervent exclamation from the monk, instantly followed by a faint cry from your mother's lips. I flew to the bed; she had raised herself from the pillow, her arms were extended, as in the act of supplication, and a celestial glow irradiated her dying features. The priest stood in an attitude of eager attention: his cowl was removed; and, judge of my sensations, when I recognized the countenance of De Courcy!"

"My father!" exclaimed Luciè; "that priest" —

"Wait, and you shall know all;" interrupted Madame de la Tour. "That priest was indeed your father; he had taken the vows of a rigid order, and Providence guided him to the death-bed of your mother. I pass over the scene which followed; it is too hallowed for description. Suffice it to say, the solemn confession of that dreadful moment convinced him of her innocence, and her last sufferings were soothed by mutual reconciliation and forgiveness. Your father closed her eyes in their last sleep, and pressing you for an instant to his heart, rushed almost frantic from the convent.

"On the following day, my father sought De Courcy at the monastery, hoping to draw him back to the world by the touching claims of parental love. But he had already left it, never to return; and the superior had sworn to conceal his new abode from every human being. Before leaving the convent, on the night of your mother's death, he confirmed her bequest, which had already given you to my eldest sister, then a rigid Catholic. But my father soon after became a convert to the opinions of the Hugonots, to which we also inclined; and my sister's marriage with M. Rossville confirmed her in those sentiments. She thought proper to educate you in a faith which she had adopted from deliberate conviction; and, as your father had renounced his claims, she of course felt responsible only to her own conscience. Every effort to find him, indeed, continued unavailing; years passed away, and by all who had known him he was numbered as with the dead.

"But your father still lived, Luciè, and the recollection of his injured wife forever haunted him; her misery, her untimely death, all weighed heavily on his conscience, and he sought to expiate his crime by a life of austerity, and the most constant and painful acts of self-denial and devotion. Yet the severest penance which he inflicted on himself was to renounce his child, to burst the ties of natural affection, that no earthly claims might interfere with those holy duties to which he had consecrated his future life."

"Just heavens!" said Luciè, with emotion; "could such a sacrifice be exacted? dearest aunt, tell me if he yet lives, if I am right" —

"He does live," interrupted Madame de la Tour; "he received permission to quit his monastery only to fulfil a more rigid vow, which bound him to a life of unremitting hardship; and, after a severe illness, that for several weeks deprived him of reason, he at length reached this new world, where for nearly twenty years" —

"Father Gilbert!" exclaimed Luciè, starting from her seat in powerful agitation.

"Yes," said a deep, solemn voice; and the dark form of the priest, who had entered unnoticed, stood beside her; "my child, behold your father!"

"My father!" repeated Luciè, as she rushed into his extended arms, and sunk weeping upon his bosom.

CHAPTER XXI.

Come, bright Improvement! on the car of Time.
And rule the spacious world from clime to clime:
Thy handmaid arts shall every wild explore,
Trace every wave, and culture every shore.
CAMPBELL.

The tempered beams of a September sun glanced mildly on the quiet shores of the Massachusetts, and tinged with mellowed hues the richness of its autumnal scenery. It was on that holy day, which our puritan ancestors were wont to regard emphatically as a "day of rest;" and nature seemed hushed to a repose as deep and expressive as on that first earthly sabbath when God finished his creative work, and "saw that it was very good." The public worship of the morning was ended; and the citizens of Boston were dispersing through the different streets and avenues of the town, to their various places of abode. The mass which issued from the portal of the sanctuary with grave and orderly demeanor, appeared to melt away as one by one, or in household groups, they turned aside to their respective dwellings, till all gradually disappeared, and the streets were again left silent and deserted.

Arthur Stanhope had withdrawn from the crowd, and stood alone on the margin of the bay, which curved its broad basin around the peninsula of Boston. He had received no tidings from St. John's, since the day he quitted it; and, with extreme impatience, he awaited the return of a small trading vessel, which was hourly expected from thence. But his eyes vainly traversed the wide expanse of water; all around it blended with the bright blue sky, and no approaching bark darkened its unruffled surface. Silence reigned over the scene as undisturbed as when the adventurous pilgrims first leaped upon the inhospitable shore. But it was the silence of that hallowed rest which man offered in homage to his creator, not that primeval calm which then brooded over the savage wilderness. Time, since the day on which they took possession, had caused the waste places to "rejoice, and the desert to blossom as a rose." The land to which they fled from the storms of persecution had become a pleasant abode; and their interests and affections were detached from the parent country, and fixed on the home of their adoption.

The tide of emigration ceased with the triumph of the puritan cause in England; but the early colonists had already laid deep the broad foundations on which the fabric of civil and religious liberty was reared. Prudence and persevering zeal had conquered the first and most arduous labors of the settlement; and they looked forward with pious confidence to its future prosperity, firmly persuaded that God had reserved it for the resting place of his chosen people. The rugged soil yielded to the hand of industry, and brought forth its treasures. The shores of the bay no longer presented a scene of wild and solitary magnificence. Forests, which had defied the blasts of ages, were swept away; and, in their stead, fields of waving grain hung their golden ears in the ripening sun, ready for the coming harvest. Flocks and herds grazed in the green pastures which sloped to the water's edge, or collected in meditative groups beneath the scattered trees that spread their ample branches to shelter them. The noble range of hills which rose beyond in beautiful inequalities, girdling the indented coast, presented a rich and variegated prospect. Broad patches of cultivation appeared in every sheltered nook, and tracts of smooth mown grass relieved the eye from the midst of sterile wilds. Luxuriant corn-fields fringed the borders of hanging woodlands, which clothed the steep acclivities; and on the boldest summits wide regions were laid bare, where the adventurous axe had broken the dark line of frowning forests, and prepared the way for future culture. Here and there a thriving village burst upon the view, its clustering houses interspersed with gardens and orchards of young fruit trees.

The infant capital, from its central and commanding situation, rose pre-eminent above the sister settlements. It had prospered beyond the hopes of the most sanguine, and was already a mart for the superfluous products of the colony. That regard to order and decorum, displayed by the magistrates in their earliest regulations, and a uniformity in the distribution of land for streets and dwelling lots, had prevented much confusion, as the population increased. Its limits were then comparatively narrow; man had not yet encroached on the dominions of the sea to extend the boundaries of the peninsula. Where the first wharves were erected, broad and busy streets now traverse almost the centre of the city; and fuel was gathered, and wild animals hunted, from the woods that grew in abundance on the neck, which is now a protracted and populous avenue to the adjoining country. Extensive marshes skirted the borders of the river Charles, and the three hills which formed its prominent natural features were steep and rugged cliffs. One, indeed, was surmounted by a wind-mill, which for many years labored unceasingly for the public good, and ably supplied a deficiency of water-mills; and another, which overlooked the harbor, was defended by a few pieces of artillery; thus early betraying that jealous vigilance which has ever distinguished the people of New-England. The last, and most lofty, was still a barren waste, descending into the humid fens which are now converted into a beautiful common, the only ornamental promenade which our metropolis can boast.

Improvement was for a time necessarily gradual. Religion, the only motive which could have induced such sacrifices as were made in its cause, was first established; and civil order, and the means of education, were deemed next important by the wise and virtuous founders of our republic. The necessaries and comforts of life were secured before they had leisure to think of its embellishments. Necessity produced a frugal and industrious spirit, and the wealthiest encouraged by their example the economy and self-denial of the lower orders. Artisans and mechanics soon found ample employment, and various manufactures were ingeniously contrived to supply the ordinary wants of the colony. The natural products of the soil gradually yielded a superfluity, which was exported to the West Indian and other islands; — the commencement of that extensive traffic, which has since raised Boston to a high rank among the commercial cities of the world. It was also sent in exchange for the commodities of the mother country, who, indulgent to her children while too feeble to dispute her authority, then generously remitted those duties which afterwards proved a "root of bitterness" between them. The fisheries, also, were even then an object of consideration; and many found employment in that craft, which has now become a source of national wealth. Vessels of considerable burthen were launched from the shores of the wilderness, and their light keels already parted the waters of distant seas. Nations which then viewed our hardy navigators with contempt, have since seen their white sails flutter in the winds of every climate, and their adventurous ships braving the dangers of every rugged shore. The proudest have acknowledged their rights in each commercial port, and the bravest have struck unwillingly to their victorious flag.

The advancement which the colony had made within fourteen years from its settlement, was indeed surprising. The germ of future prosperity seemed bursting from its integuments. The principles of a free government were established; the seed which was "sown in tears," though it appeared "the least of all seeds," was preparing to shoot forth and spread its branches into a mighty tree. As yet, however, the future was "hid under a cloud;" and what had already been done, could only be justly appreciated by those who acted and suffered from the commencement. But the fruits of their labor were evident, even to the most indifferent observer; and Stanhope's thoughts were forcibly drawn from the subject of his own anxiety, and fixed on the scene before him.

The scene, glorious as it appeared in the simple garniture of nature, and softened by the adornments of art, charmed the eye and awakened the enthusiasm of a refined and imaginative mind. But the high moral courage, the stern yet lofty impulse of duty, which had achieved so great an enterprize; which had burst the strong links of kindred and country, and exchanged honor and affluence for reproach and poverty, and the countless trials of a wilderness, appealed directly to the best feelings of the heart. Arthur was reminded by all around him, of this noble triumph of mind and principle over the greatest physical obstacles; and he strongly felt the contrast which it presented to the habits and opinions of the Acadian settlers, with whom he had been lately associated. The bitter enmity of La Tour and D'Aulney, the struggle for pre-eminence, which kept them continually at strife, had deadened every social affection and aroused the most fierce and selfish passions. They had attempted to colonize a portion of the New World, from interested and ambitious motives; their followers were in general actuated by a hope of gain, or the mere spirit of adventure, which characterized that age; and, if religion was at all considered, it was only from motives of policy. The purity and disinterestedness of the New-England fathers was more striking from the comparison; and, as Stanhope mused on them, he wondered that the light sacrifices he had himself been compelled to make, could ever have appeared so important. His country, his profession, his hopes of honorable advancement, were indeed abandoned; but dearer hopes had succeeded the dreams of ambition; and what country would not become a paradise, when brightened by the smiles of affection!

His reverie, by a very loverlike process, had thus revolved back to the point where it commenced, when he was reminded of the lapse of time, by the sound of a bell, which floated sweetly on the still air, and announced the stated hour for the second services of the day. He was slowly turning to obey its summons, when his attention was attracted by the appearance of a vessel; and he again paused in curiosity and suspense. It was a pinnace of large size, and sailed slowly over the smooth waters, frequently tacking to catch the light breeze, which scarcely swelled the canvass. The waves curled, as if in sport, around the prow, leaving a sinuous track behind, as it came up through the channel, north of Castle

Island, like a solitary bird, skimming the surface of the deep, and spreading its snowy wings towards some region of rest. As it entered the spacious harbor, the gay streamer, which hung idly from the mainmast, was raised by a passing breeze, displaying the colors of France, united with the private arms of Mons. d'Aulney.

The vessel soon attracted general observation, but the sanctity of the day prevented any open expression of curiosity or surprise. It was permitted to anchor, unmolested by the formidable battery on the eastern hill; the bell continued to ring for public worship, and the citizens to assemble as usual. But, situated as the colonists then were, with regard to Acadia, the arrival of a vessel from thence, was a matter of some importance. Certain negociations had already taken place between the magistrates of Boston and M. d'Aulney, and the latter had proposed sending commissioners to arrange a treaty. The magistrates, rightly conjecturing that they had at length arrived, sent two officers to receive them at the water's side, and conduct them quietly to an inn. Wishing, however, to treat them with suitable respect, when the services of the day were over, a guard of musketeers was despatched to escort them to the governor's house, where they were invited to remain, during their stay in town.

A treaty was commenced on the following day; and, throughout its progress, the utmost ceremony and attention was observed towards the commissioners, which policy or politeness could suggest. Mutual aggressions were complained of, and mutual concessions made; and though D'Aulney had, in truth, been hitherto faithless to his promises, the Bostonians evidently feared his growing power, and strongly inclined to conciliatory measures. Under these circumstances, an amnesty was, without much difficulty, concluded; and the commissioners soon after returned, well satisfied, to Penobscot.

This treaty, for a time, seemed almost fatal to the prospects of La Tour. It restrained the colonists from rendering him any further assistance; and there was every probability that D'Aulney would at length effect his long meditated designs against fort St. John's. Stanhope felt much anxiety respecting Luciè's situation; but as winter was now rapidly approaching, it was hardly possible that any hostile operations would be commenced, before the return of spring. That period, he trusted, would fulfil the hopes which she had sanctioned, and place her under his own protection; and, through the autumn, he had the satisfaction of hearing frequently from her, by means of the vessels which continued to trade at the river, with La Tour. With extreme surprise, he learned that she had discovered her father, in the mysterious priest; and, strange as the connection seemed, he felt a satisfaction, in knowing that she could claim a natural guardian, till he was permitted to remove her from a situation, which was so constantly exposed to danger.

CHAPTER XXII.

The wars are over,
  The spring is come;
The bride and her lover
  Have sought their home:
They are happy, we rejoice;
Let their hearts have an echo in every voice!

LORD BYRON.

Never did months revolve more slowly, than through that winter, to the impatient Stanhope. During its inclemency, all communication with the French settlements ceased, and he, of course, heard nothing of Luciè, — a suspension of intercourse which was almost insupportable. By the earliest approach of spring, however, the traders and fishermen again adventured their barks on the stormy bay of Fundy, and the icy shores of Newfoundland. Boston harbor, which had been sealed, for several months, by the severe cold, then characteristic of the climate, was freed by the bright sun and genial gales of that vernal season. Numerous vessels floated on its dancing waves; and all around, the adjacent shores were teeming with sights and sounds of rural industry.

It was shortly rumored, that M. d'Aulney was preparing to attack fort St. John's; some even affirmed, that his vessels had already been seen, hovering near the entrance of the river. Stanhope's extreme anxiety could brook no farther delay; and, under such circumstances, he felt acquitted of the obligation which Luciè's request had imposed on him, and at liberty to anticipate a few weeks of the time appointed for his return to her. Early in April, therefore, he embarked in a neat pinnace, and after a short voyage, reached the rugged coast of Acadia. Daylight was closing, as he approached St. John's; but fortunately the clear twilight served to show him the changes which had taken place there. Several armed vessels blockaded the river, and the standard of M. d'Aulney waved triumphantly from the walls of the fort.

These signs of conquest could not be mistaken: the late haughty possessor had evidently suffered defeat; but what fate had overtaken him, and where had his family found a refuge? Luciè, the sharer of their fortunes, — where should he seek her? was the most anxious thought of Stanhope; and painful solicitude checked the tide of joyous expectation which he had so sanguinely indulged. Hoping to obtain information from some peasant in the neighborhood, he anchored a few miles below the fort, and throwing himself into a small boat, proceeded alone to a well-remembered landing-place. He steered his bark cautiously along the shores of the bay, which were already darkened by the evening shadows; and, rowing with all his strength, soon reached the destined spot, and sprang eagerly upon the strand. Ascending an eminence, the country opened widely around him; the smoke curled quietly from the scattered cottages, and the scene was unchanged since he last saw it, except from the variation of the seasons. The fields, which were then crowned with the riches of autumn, had since been seared by wintry frosts, which now slowly relaxed their rigid grasp. Faint streaks of verdure began to tinge the sunny valleys, though patches of snow still lingered within their cold recesses. A thousand silver rills burst from the moistened earth, and leaped down the sloping banks, chiming, in soft concert, with the evening breeze. Every swelling bud exhaled the perfumed breath of spring; and all nature seemed awake to welcome her bland approach.

The peasantry of the country were evidently unmolested, and probably cared little for the change of masters. Arthur had, as yet, seen no living being; and he hastened to Annette's cottage, which stood at a short distance, half hid by the matted foliage of some sheltering pines. It no longer wore the air of open hospitality, which once distinguished it; the gay voice of its mistress ever carolling at her labour, was silent, and the closed door and casements seemed to portend some sad reverse. Stanhope paused an instant; and as he leaned against a rude fence which enclosed the garden plat, his eye rested on a slender mound of earth, covered with fresh sods, and surrounded by saplings of willow, newly planted. It was evidently a grave; and, with a chilled heart, and excited feelings, he leaped the slight enclosure, fearing, he knew not, dared not ask himself, what unknown evil.

At that moment, he heard light approaching footsteps; he turned and saw a female advancing slowly, and too much engrossed by her own thoughts to have yet observed him. He could not be deceived; he sprang to meet her, repeating the name of "Luciè;" and an eager exclamation of "Stanhope, is it possible!" expressed her joyful recognition.

"Why are you so pale and pensive, dear Luciè," asked Stanhope, regarding her with solicitude, when the first rapturous emotions had subsided; "and what brings you to this melancholy spot at such a lonely hour?"

"Oh, Arthur," she replied, "you know not half the changes which have taken place since you were here, or you would not ask why I am pale and pensive! this is the grave of my kindest relative; till you came, I almost thought of my last friend!"

"Good heavens! of your aunt, Luciè; of Madame de la Tour?"

A burst of tears, which she could no longer restrain, was Luciè's answer; her feelings had, of late, been severely tried, and it was many moments before her own exertions, or the soothings of affection succeeded in calming her emotions. A long conversation ensued; each had much to say, and Luciè, in particular, many events to communicate. But as the narrative was often interrupted by question and remark, and delayed by the expression of those hopes and sentiments which lovers are wont to intersperse in their discourse, we shall omit such superfluities, and sum up, as briefly as possible, all that is necessary to elucidate our story.

Madame de la Tour's constitution was too delicate to bear the rigor of a northern climate, and from her first arrival in Acadia, her health began almost imperceptibly to decline. She never entirely recovered from the severe indisposition which attacked her in the autumn, though the vigor and cheerfulness of her mind long resisted the depressing influence of disease. But she was perfectly aware of her danger even before the bloom faded from her cheek sufficiently to excite the alarm of those around her. It was a malady which had proved fatal to many of her family; and she had too often witnessed its insidious approaches in others, to be deceived when she was herself the victim. Towards the close of winter, she was confined entirely to her apartment, and Luciè, and the faithful Annette, were her kind and unwearied attendants. Her decline was from that time rapid, but it was endured with a fortitude which had distinguished her in every situation of life. Still young, and with much to render existence pleasant and desirable, she met its close with cheerful resignation, surrounded by the weeping objects of her love. On Luciè's affectionate heart her untimely death left a deep and lasting impression. She felt desolate indeed, thus deprived of the only relative, with whom she could claim connexion and sympathy.

The parental tie so lately discovered, and which had opened to Luciè a new spring of tenderness, became a source of painful anxiety. Father Gilbert, — so we shall still call him, — had yielded for a brief season to the indulgence of those natural feelings, which were awakened by the recognition of his daughter. But his ascetic habits, and the blind bigotry of his creed, soon regained their influence over his mind, and led him to distrust the most virtuous emotions of his heart. The self-inflicted penance, which estranged him from her, in infancy, he deemed still binding; and the vow which he had taken to lead a life of devotion, he thought no circumstances could annul. As the priest of God, he must conquer every earthly passion; the work to which he was dedicated yet remained unaccomplished, and the sins of his early life were still unatoned.

Thus he reasoned, blinded by the false dogmas of a superstitious creed; and the arguments of Madame de la Tour, the tears and entreaties of Luciè, had been alike disregarded. The return of the priest, who usually officiated at the fort, was the signal for him to depart on a tour of severe duty to the most distant settlements of Acadia. Nothing could change his determination; he parted from Luciè with much emotion, solemnly conjuring her to renounce her spiritual errors, and embrace the faith of the only true church. As his child, he assured her, he should pray for her happiness, as a heretic, for her conversion; but he relinquished the authority of a father, which his profession forbade him to exercise, and left her to the guidance of her own conscience. From that time, Luciè had neither seen nor heard from him; but solicitude for his fate pressed heavily on her heart, and she shed many secret and bitter tears for her unfortunate parent.

Soon after the death of Madame de la Tour, Luciè removed her residence to the cottage of Annette. The fort was no longer a suitable or pleasant abode for her. Mons. de la Tour disregarded the wishes which his lady had expressed in her last illness, — that Luciè might be allowed to follow her own inclinations, — and renewed his endeavours to force her into a marriage with De Valette. But his threats and persuasions were both firmly resisted, and proved equally ineffectual to accomplish his purpose. De Valette, indeed, had too much pride and generosity to urge his suit after a decided rejection; and he was vexed by his uncle's selfish pertinacity. In the early period of his attachment to Luciè, he accidentally discovered that most of her fortune had become involved in the private speculations of her guardian, and was probably lost to her. But he often declared, that he asked no dowry with such a bride, and if he could obtain her hand, he should never seek redress for the patrimony she had lost. La Tour, conscious that he had wronged her, and fearing that no other suitor would prove equally disinterested, was on that account anxious to promote a union, which would so easily free him from the penalty of his offence.

Early in the spring, La Tour left St. John's for Newfoundland, hoping to obtain such assistance from Sir David Kirk, who was then commanding there, as would enable him to retain possession of his fort. He was accompanied by De Valette, who intended to sail from thence for his native country. It was not till after their departure, that Luciè learned the reduced state of her finances from Jacques, the husband of Annette, who had long enjoyed the confidence of his lord, and been conversant with his pecuniary affairs. She was naturally vexed and indignant at the heartless and unprincipled conduct of her guardian; though there was a romantic pleasure in the idea, that it would only test, more fully, the strength and constancy of Stanhope's attachment. Woman is seldom selfish or ambitious in her affection; Luciè loved, and she felt still rich in the possession of a true and virtuous heart.

The absence of La Tour was eagerly embraced by D'Aulney, as a favorable opportunity to accomplish his meditated designs. Scarcely had the former doubled Cape Sable, when his enemy sailed up the bay with a powerful force, and anchored before St. John's. The intimidated garrison made barely a show of resistance, and the long contested fort was surrendered without a struggle. D'Aulney treated the conquered with a lenity, which won many to his cause; and he permitted the neighboring inhabitants to remain undisturbed on a promise of submission, which was readily accorded to him.

Mr. Broadhead, the chaplain of Madame de la Tour, found refuge in the cottage of Annette, who charitably disregarded religious prejudices, and treated him with the utmost kindness and attention, from respect to the memory of her mistress. But, having lost the protection of his patroness, he could no longer, as he said, "consent to sojourn in the tents of the ungodly idolaters," and meditated a return to Scotland. To facilitate this object, he gladly accepted a passage in Stanhope's vessel to Boston; from whence, it was probable, he might soon find an opportunity to recross the Atlantic. The same reasons induced Jacques and Annette also to become their fellow-passengers; they were wearied of the toil and uncertainty inseparable from a new settlement, and sighed for the humble pleasures they had once enjoyed among the gay peasantry of France.

Every thing thus satisfactorily explained and arranged, no obstacle remained to delay the marriage of Stanhope and Luciè. The ceremony was accordingly performed by Mr. Broadhead; and they immediately bade a last farewell to the wild regions of Acadia. Clear skies and favorable gales, present enjoyment, and the bright hopes of futurity, rendered their short voyage delightful, and seemed the happy presage of a calm and prosperous life. Stanhope, with the fond pride of gratified affection, presented his bride to his expecting parents; and never was a daughter received with more cordiality and tenderness. They had known and loved her, in the pleasant abode of their native land; and their maturer judgments sanctioned his youthful choice. Every succeeding year strengthened their confidence and attachment; her sweetness and vivacity, her exemplary goodness and devotion to her husband, created a union of feeling and interest, which was the joy of their declining years.

The happiness of Arthur and Luciè was permanent; and, if not wholly exempted from the evils which ever cling to this state of trial, their virtuous principles were an unfailing support, their mutual tenderness, an exhaustless consolation. The wealth and distinction, which once courted them, were unregretted; the green vales of England, and the vine-covered hills of France, lingered in their remembrance, only as a bright and fleeting vision. It was their ambition to fulfil the duties of moral and intellectual beings; and the rugged climate of New-England became the chosen home of their affections.

We feel pledged, by the rules of honorable authorship, to satisfy any curiosity which may exist, respecting the remaining characters of our narrative; and if the reader's interest is already wearied, he is at liberty to omit this brief, concluding paragraph.

De Valette embarked at Newfoundland, in a vessel bound for some English port, which was driven by stress of weather, on the Irish coast. The crew barely escaped with their lives, and the young Frenchman, by a freak of fortune, was thrown upon the hospitality of a gentleman, who cultivated an hereditary estate in the vicinity. The kind urgency of his host could not be resisted; and the attractions of an only child bade fair to heal the wounds which Luciè's coldness had inflicted. His stay was protracted from day to day; and in short with the usual constancy of despairing lovers, — he soon learned to think the fair daughter of the "emerald isle" even more charming than the dark-eyed maiden of his own sunny clime. Her smiles were certainly more encouraging; and, at the end of a few weeks, De Valette led her to the bridal altar.

La Tour was disappointed in his application to Sir David Kirk, and, for a time, his tide of fortune seemed entirely to have ebbed. He again visited Boston, but did not meet with a very cordial reception, though a few merchants entrusted him with a considerable sum of money, on some private speculation. This he disposed of, in his own way, and never took the trouble to render any account, or make the least restitution to the owners. The death of D'Aulney, however, which happened in the course of a few years, reversed his prospects, and reinstated him in all his possessions. He was firmly established in the sole government of Acadia; and, soon after, he contracted a second marriage with the object of his early affection, — the still beautiful widow of M. d'Aulney. With no rival to dispute his authority, his remaining life was passed in tranquillity; the colony, relieved from strife and contention, began to flourish, and his descendants for many years enjoyed their inheritance unmolested.

Arthur Stanhope, a few months after his union with Luciè, was appointed the agent of some public business, which required a voyage to Pemaquid. The recollection of father Gilbert forcibly recurred to him, when he found himself so near the shores of Mount Desart, — a place which the priest had frequented, probably for its very loneliness, or perhaps, from some peculiar associations. It was possible he might again find him there, or hear some tidings which would relieve Luciè's anxiety respecting him; and, in this hope, he one day sought its sequestered shades. The sun was declining, when he moored his little bark, and proceeded alone through the same path, which he remembered, on a former occasion, to have trodden. The open plain soon burst upon his view; and, to his surprise, the prostrate wooden cross was again erected in the midst of it. A figure knelt at its foot; Arthur approached, — the tall, attenuated form, the dark, flowing garments could not be mistaken; — it was indeed father Gilbert. Supposing him engaged in some act of devotion, Stanhope waited several moments, silent, and unwilling to disturb him. But he continued perfectly motionless; — Arthur advanced still closer; — one hand grasped the cross, the other held a small crucifix, which he always wore suspended from his neck. A glow of [Transcriber's Note: Word illegible in original] rested on his pale features; his eyes were closed, and a triumphant smile lingered on his parted lips. Arthur started, and his blood chilled as he gazed at him; he touched his hand, — it was cold and stiff; — he pressed his fingers on his heart, — it had ceased to beat! — Father Gilbert was no more!

The spirit seemed to have just burst its weary bondage, and without a struggle; the grassy turf was his dying couch, and the breeze of the desert sighed a requiem for his departing soul!

THE END.

www.ingramcontent.com/pod-product-compliance
Lightning Source LLC
Chambersburg PA
CBHW050756250626
47155CB00005B/2090